"I was a teenage ski widow..."

I took the phone into the hall closet for privacy and was all ready to give Tim an update on the day's new members in the detention club, when he started talking about bindings and moguls and stem christies till I wanted to scream. So I did. Of course I was sorry the instant I did it, but the scream had already started before my brain kicked in to inform me that I was doing something majorly stupid.

Other Bullseye Books you will enjoy

And the Other, Gold by Susan Wojciechowski
The Ghost Inside the Monitor
   by Margaret J. Anderson
Marci's Secret Book of Flirting (Don't Go Out
   Without It!) by Jan Gelman
Not on a White Horse by Nancy Springer
Witch Week by Diana Wynne Jones

Patty Dillman of Hot Dog Fame

●

Susan Wojciechowski

To Travis —
Hope you find this
book "delicious"!

Susan Wojciechowski

BULLSEYE BOOKS • ALFRED A. KNOPF
NEW YORK

November, 1993

Library of Congress Catalog Card Number: 88-22565
ISBN: 0-679-80170-7
RL: 5.1
First Bullseye edition: November 1990

Manufactured in the United States of America
10 9 8 7 6 5 4 3 2 1

With love
for Paul
who likes his hot dogs with ketchup and onions

Patty Dillman of Hot Dog Fame

1 The big, round clock above the blackboard read 10:59 A.M. My scalp started to prickle. 11:00. My heart began to pound. 11:01. Every pore of my body started to sweat. In exactly four minutes I would raise my hand to ask if I could leave religion class and go to the girls' room. I would meet Tracy there and we would attempt the most daring adventure of our ten-year career as best friends.

Tracy and I met in a nursery school car pool when we were three. The first thing she did was teach me to stuff Hershey's Kiss wrappers up my nose and she's been talking me into dumb stunts ever since. They all seem like good ideas at the time.

This most recent "great idea" came in a blinding flash while we were in our school play, *Oklahoma!* a few weeks ago. Father Damian, the director, wore a different wild hat at every rehearsal. Once he wore one with a flashing red light on top, once he wore moose antlers, and once he wore a plastic helmet with a tricycle wheel on it that spun around when he moved.

When we heard from one of the boys in the play that Father had a whole wall full of hats in his room, we knew we couldn't live through eighth grade without seeing that collection for ourselves.

Of course, the location of Father's room was a problem. In our school, Saint Ignatius Junior High, the boys have their classes on one side of the building and the girls have theirs on the other. The third floor, where the nuns and priests on the faculty live, is called Never-Never Land. The girls are warned never, never even to think about going near the nuns' rooms. This is practically rule number one of the ninety-nine thousand rules we have to memorize. However, nobody ever thought to tell us not to go near the priests' rooms.

"So we aren't really breaking a rule," Tracy reasoned, as we planned our strategy.

I told Tracy I wasn't sure the principal would agree.

"Well then, we won't ask the principal to go with us," Tracy said.

We decided that on the last day of school before Thanksgiving vacation, while the whole student body was in the auditorium for Mass, we could sneak over to the boys' side of school, slink up to Never-Never Land, look at the hats, sneak back down, and get to the girls' side unnoticed. Are we dumb or what?

11:02. I fidgeted in my seat, nervously biting my nails and forcing myself to pay attention as the teacher explained our latest religion assignment.

She was droning on about how we had not only to memorize the corporal works of mercy, we actually had to *do* one and write a paper about it.

As she was listing the works of mercy on the board—visit the sick, shelter the homeless, feed the hungry—I looked up again at the clock. 11:05. I wiped my damp palms down the sides of my uniform skirt and raised my hand.

"Patricia?" asked Sister Clarabelle. Her name is really Sister Barbara Clare but she has a big red nose so we call her Clarabelle the Clown behind her back.

"Could I go to the girls' room, Sister?" My throat was so tight I could barely squeak the words out.

"I'm sorry. It will have to wait. I was just about to ask you girls to line up and proceed to the auditorium for Mass."

"It's an emergency!" I pleaded, suddenly realizing that the whole plan would go down the tubes if Sister Clarabelle didn't let me go to the girls' room. She's probably the oldest, strictest and most suspicious nun on the planet earth.

"An extreme emergency!" I added for good measure.

Sister Clarabelle sighed and said, "Go ahead then. But please try to be unobtrusive when you come marching down the aisle of the auditorium to join us."

Actually Tracy and I had decided that if we returned alive we'd just slither into the back row, unobtrusively of course.

"And," Sister Clarabelle added, so sternly that I stopped in my tracks, "I want you back in five minutes or I shall send the bloodhounds after you!"

I gulped. "Why is she always so darn suspicious of me?" I mumbled under my breath as I broke into a run.

"Walk!" I heard her call out from behind the closed classroom door. I swear she has unnatural powers.

I walked.

When I got to the first floor girls' room Tracy was waiting for me, sitting on the long shelf under the mirror that's meant to hold purses and books. At least once a week during PA announcements we're warned not to sit on the shelves because they weren't built to bear heavy weight, but we all sit on them anyway. They're practically the only place to sit in the bathrooms.

I couldn't believe how calm Tracy looked, her long legs stretched out on the ledge in front of her as if she didn't have a care in the world.

Tracy is gorgeous without even trying. It's absolutely disgusting. She doesn't wear any makeup, not even lipstick. Not like me. I put on lip gloss and blush to empty the trash. And Tracy usually wears her incredibly long blonde hair in a single braid, which she was twirling, like she always does when she's concentrating. She had the totally angelic look on her face which warns people who know her that she's up to no good.

When I walked into the girls' room I was panting with fear. Tracy swung her legs down and hopped off the shelf. "Slow, deep breaths," she ordered. I inhaled, then blew out a stream of air through pursed lips while Tracy waited patiently.

She's like that. I hyperventilate, and she acts as if we're about to go for a stroll through the park.

As usual I had last-minute cold feet. I was about to suggest that we quit while we were ahead when Tracy said very calmly, "I think we can do it. Everyone is going to Mass, and I mean everyone. I even saw the janitor go into the auditorium. Let's move."

Tracy swung the door open and stuck her head out. I grabbed her braid and pulled her back inside. "Let's go over the plan one more time," I said, stalling.

"You're stalling," Tracy accused.

"I am not stalling. I just want to be sure we're doing the right thing." I walked over to the mirror and started running my fingers through the stubborn brown waves around my face.

"Of course we're not doing the right thing," she said, exasperated. "If we were doing the right thing we'd be in the auditorium at this moment singing 'Lord Have Mercy.' But come on Pats, you only go around once in life so don't wimp out on me now."

"I have no intention of wimping out on you. I just want to wait a couple more minutes till we're sure everyone is in the auditorium." I sat down on the ledge and started biting my nails.

Tracy ignored me. She threw her shoulders back and marched into the hall like she owned the place.

I caught the bathroom door just before it shut and followed meekly.

"Patty," she barked at me, "will you please loosen your death grip on my arm? My fingers are going numb." She pried my hand away and massaged her fingers as we walked.

We went down the hall, passed the main lobby and kept going. My eyes were riveted on the door ahead of me, the door to the boys' side.

Tracy flung it open confidently and kept going, straight down the front hall to the stairway at the far end. The place was so quiet you could hear my shoes squeaking with every step I took.

"What if some teacher sees us?" I whispered, slowing my pace. "Or one of the boys? Or . . ." I sucked in my breath as the horrible thought occurred to me, "What if Tim sees us?"

The thought of my boyfriend seeing me made the whole plan suddenly seem dumb. He'd think I was an airbrain if he ever found out, and he'd be embarrassed to be my boyfriend after that. I decided I'd rather die.

Tracy grabbed my arm and pulled it practically out of its socket. "Tim is not going to see you. Nobody is going to see you. Just me. And someday we're going to get rich writing a book about our exciting lives. Now come on, partner." She punched me in the arm and ran up the metal-edged stairs two at a time. I followed.

At the second floor we peered up to the double

8

doors one flight higher—the doors to Never-Never Land. I felt a sudden rush of excitement. Tracy and I looked at each other. Then we broke into grins and raced each other to the top.

Tracy pulled open one of the heavy doors. My heart was thumping so wildly I could feel my eardrums pulsating. But I took a deep breath, stepped beyond the door and flattened myself against the wall, as if that would make me invisible.

My eyes swept across Never-Never Land. It didn't look anything like what I had expected. I had thought it would be cold and institutional with tile walls and gray speckled linoleum floors, and have holy pictures all over the walls. Instead, the walls were covered with pale blue striped wallpaper and the floor was covered with thick grayish-blue carpeting. Near us was a row of doors on both sides of the hall, which we figured were to the bedrooms. At the far end were two archways, one opening onto a living room jam-packed with easy chairs and two couches, and the other onto a dining room. There was no sign of life.

Luckily we knew more or less where Father Damian's room was. The guy who told us about the wall of hats sort of remembered its location because he'd had to help carry a desk up to Father Damian's room in September. For two dollars he had told us that it was four or five doors down the hall, on the right.

We found the room without any trouble. It was

the only room without the door shut. Tracy and I slipped inside and crouched behind a chair in the corner.

"Holy ravioli!" Tracy whispered.

"Ditto," I answered, my eyes bugging out of my head.

We stayed crouched there for a while, mesmerized by the sight of the hats. There was a coonskin cap, an Indian headdress, a policeman's hat, a black silk top hat . . . there were hats from one end of the room to the other, and from ceiling to floor. It was totally awesome.

After a couple of minutes, Tracy pulled her camera out of her purse and took a few pictures, and we beat it out of there.

"We did it! We did it!" the two of us mouthed silently to each other when we were back in the hall. I grabbed Tracy's hand and squeezed it. She punched me in the arm. Then we slowly began our descent. Halfway down the stairway to the second floor, it happened. Tracy's camera slipped out of her purse and fell down the steps below her with a solid "clunk, clunk, clunk."

It wasn't until Tracy had scooped it up and stuffed it back in her purse and I had grabbed the runaway roll of film that we noticed the shoes. They were huge, shiny black ones, the kind a priest might wear. Attached to them were the legs and body of Father John, the boys' principal.

"Just what in thunderation do you two young

ladies think you're doing?" He always roars, even when he thinks he's speaking quietly. But right then he roared with the force of a gale wind, and I was sure Sister Clarabelle's ears were perking up and she was looking around for me.

My mouth and brain went into instant paralysis. But Tracy stayed calm. She zipped her purse shut, looked straight at him with her big, innocent eyes and told him the truth. Well, tried to.

"We just wanted to see Father Damian's . . ." she began. But Father John interrupted.

"You just wanted to see Father Damian? You just wanted to see Father Damian? Why in thunderation didn't it occur to you to make an appointment? Why in blessed thunderation couldn't you see Father Damian in his classroom?"

Neither of us answered, so Father John hauled us over to our side of school to deposit us in the office of the girls' principal. As we walked behind Father John, all I could think of was Tim suddenly appearing out of nowhere and seeing me. I tried to keep my head down and toward the wall.

"What's the matter? You look like your neck is broken or something," Tracy whispered.

"Just shut up and don't look at me or *your* neck is gonna be broken," I hissed.

Father John deposited us in Sister Marianne's office, ordered us not so much as to blink while he was gone, and left to look for her.

"How do you spell suspended?" I whispered to

Tracy when Father John had left. Tracy twirled her braid and I bit my nails, while we waited for the firing squad to arrive. It's funny, whenever we plan our schemes, we talk about getting caught by the superpowers, but I don't think either of us had ever thought it could really happen. And now it had, and I was shaking so hard you could hear my knees knocking against each other.

Tracy looked down at my knees, then at my face. "Why are your eyes watering? You're not bawling are you?" she asked.

"I'm trying not to blink, like Father John said, but I don't think I can hold on much longer."

"For Pete's sake, Pats, he didn't mean it!"

"Well, I don't want to take any chances. There might be a hidden camera in here."

Just then the two principals got back, followed by Sister Clarabelle. She was hysterical over having misplaced me for the whole Mass.

"I discovered these two young ladies of yours," Father said haughtily, as if his young men never did anything wrong, "trying to sneak up to the priests' living quarters. They 'just wanted to see Father Damian.'" We caught the sarcastic tone in his voice. We also caught the words "trying to sneak up."

I sucked in my breath. Tracy gave me the slightest jab with her elbow. There was a shred of hope that I wouldn't need to know how to spell suspended, after all. Father had assumed we were on our way *up* the stairs, not down.

To spare you the details, I'll just say that they each got a turn chewing us out. When they finished, Sister Marianne went over to her file cabinet and took out our school records. As she skimmed through them I hoped she'd see that last year I was homeroom rep to the Student Council and won sixth place in the citywide Fire Prevention Essay Contest, and that this year I write a column for the school newspaper. I hoped she'd notice that Tracy was voted most enthusiastic last year, and came in third in high jumping at the All-county track meet last spring, and had a lead in this year's school play. I prayed she'd notice that we both make honor roll more often than not. Then she'd be sorry she was treating us like criminals.

Sister looked from Tracy to me and back to Tracy again. She wrote something in each of our folders. Finally, she looked up again and told us we had to serve two weeks of after-school detention beginning Monday.

Do you know what kinds of mutants you find in the detention room?

2 When I got home, my mother and father were waiting for me at the door. My father's speech was long and pure torture. He's an English professor and head of the English department at Easton College, so he's a professional at giving lectures. He brought up his most frequently cited fact, that as the oldest kid in the family, I'm supposed to set an example for Joel, Chris, and Mary.

My mother talked about "shame" and "embarrassment" and wanted to know how I could do such a thing to her. I couldn't see how my sneaking up to Father Damian's room had anything to do with her, but I wasn't dumb enough to say that out loud.

When they finally ran out of things to yell about, my mother said, "I don't know what we're going to do with that girl, Paul." I hate it when they do that. They talk like I'm a piece of furniture.

And Dad answered with his famous line, "These are the roots of anarchy." Then I knew he was about to start on one of his political lectures. Without thinking, I sighed. I knew it was a mistake the minute I did it, but it just sort of came out. That *really* got him mad, and he said, "All right, young lady, no going out, no telephone, no social contact until Monday morning. Now go to your room and think about what you did today, while your mother and I discuss this."

Actually I didn't mind going to my room. I like to be alone sometimes. I like to lie on my bed and think about anything that drifts into my head. And I like to sit at my old rolltop desk that Dad salvaged when Easton College was going to throw it out. I sit there and write in a spiral notebook about my life and my opinions and all the feelings that I have trouble saying out loud to anyone. I think keeping a diary is good practice for when I become a journalist. You can bet I wrote a ton about what happened and how I felt that day. Then I listened to Bruce Springsteen tapes till my father yelled up that I could come out.

It took a while to get used to being grounded, especially the telephone ban. Usually I race for the phone every time it rings so my brother Chris, who's eight, or my sister Mary, who's three, won't get to it first.

Chris is completely obnoxious. If the call is for me he always tells the caller exactly where I am and what I'm doing. He'll say, "Patty's in the bathroom putting on zit cream," or "Patty's cutting her toenails right now. I'll see if she can come to the phone." Stuff like that.

Mary answers the phone by picking it up and jabbering, usually into the wrong end of the receiver. After she tells the caller that she's "free" years old, goes on the big potty, and her favorite color is chocolate, she starts singing "Old Mac-Donald Had a Farm." If one of us comes near her to grab the phone away, she hangs up.

So when a call came during supper on Wednesday I jumped up from the table and answered it without thinking, maybe because I was busy trying to concentrate on holding my breath while I chewed my liver. Someone once told me that if you chew without breathing you can't taste anything.

I had just said "hello" when my brother Joel, who's a year younger than me, grabbed the receiver out of my hand and wagged his finger in front of my face saying, "Naughty, naughty."

The call was from my boyfriend Tim, who's a ninth grader at St. Iggie's and is on the football team, and who got to be my boyfriend by throwing a football at my face during practice a couple of months ago. Accidentally, he claims.

He's my first real boyfriend, unless you count Gary Holmes who's had a crush on me since last year, when he finally figured out the difference between boys and girls. He took me to the seventh-grade dance. Afterward he walked me to my door and I was in the middle of telling him how I'd gotten a blister on the back of my foot from my new heels, when he kissed me, right in mid sentence. Then he thought we were going steady or something. I finally had to put an item in the Personals column of our school newspaper: "To G.H.—Nancy and Sluggo will grow up and get married before I ever go steady with you. From P.D." Evidently he can't read, because he still operates under the assumption that I like him and am playing hard-to-get. He's a total airhead.

Anyway, back to Tim. I live in constant fear that he'll wake up some morning wondering how he ever got mixed up with a dweeb like me; someone who's so totally average. I'm not gorgeous; not like Whitney Wixsome at school, who has awesome blonde hair so long it once got caught in one of those chain barricades that corral you into line at the bank. One of the bank officials had to get scissors to cut her hair out of it.

And I don't have a great figure. Joel calls me "the body that hormones forgot." (He should talk.)

Also, my skin isn't always the greatest. Last fall I had a zit right at the end of my nose for two whole weeks. The only thing that made it go away was Tim hitting me in the face with the football.

On the plus side, my mom always tells me I have good, straight teeth and nice posture. Whoopie.

Tim is what you'd call a hunk. He has light brown hair, almost blond, that's a little long in the back but short over the ears, and curly (the hair not the ears). He has lots of muscles. And when he smiles he has this absolutely adorable dimple next to his mouth.

I stood next to the phone table in the front hall while Joel said to Tim, "Sorry, Patty can't talk. She screwed up majorly today and got sentenced to solitary confinement till Monday."

Pause.

"You're not going to believe this one. I mean, she must have taken two idiot pills this morning instead of one. She and her partner in crime (pause). Of course, who else? Well, the two of them tried to sneak over to our side of school and break into Never-Never Land. I hope the janitor disinfects our halls before we go back."

Pause.

"Who knows? I've given up trying to figure out what goes on in the black hole of her mind." I was standing in front of Joel shaking my fist at him and glaring. But he just grinned and went on, "They got detention for two weeks. At least the halls of St. Iggie's will be safe for that long."

Pause.

"Okay, I'll tell her. So long."

The minute he hung up I started pounding Joel on the back with my fists. "Joel, how could you tell him all that stuff? I hate you. Does he think I'm a dweeb? Did he laugh? Did he sound like he was embarrassed? Why did you have to mention about the detention? What did he say to tell me? Is it something awful? Don't even tell me, if it is. I don't want to know. Does he ever want to speak to me again? Tell me!"

Joel sat down at the table. He picked up his fork and started eating in that disgusting way he has of holding his fork like a shovel and stuffing food into his mouth like he's a robot with his button jammed on overdrive.

"Well, what did he want you to tell me?" I screeched.

"Oh, that," Joel said through a mouthful of green beans, salad, and fruit cocktail.

"Swallow before you talk, please," my mother interrupted.

So Joel deliberately chewed and chewed just to annoy me.

"I hope you gag," I said sweetly. He smiled and kept chewing. After a few minutes he swallowed and said, "If I had gagged you would never have known what Tim said, which was: 'Tell her Happy Thanksgiving and I'll be thinking of her this weekend while I'm in Canada searching for snow.' " Joel recommenced his food shoveling.

Chris chimed in with a grin, "And Tim said to give Patty a big kiss and a hug and tell her he's in love with her, didn't he?" He tried to give a Joel a wink.

Joel turned to Chris and said, "You're a pervert. You know that?"

"What did he say about me going to Never-Never Land?" I asked, squirming in my chair.

"He said you now qualify for the Olympic moron competition."

"Thanks, Joel. I needed that."

"No, really, he didn't say much. Believe me, Patty, nothing you do surprises anyone."

"Har-har."

I was disappointed I didn't get to talk to Tim, but

at least I found out before he left on a Thanksgiving trip that he wasn't mad at me for doing a stupid thing like getting caught at the door to Never-Never Land.

He was going on a four-day ski trip with his family, someplace far enough north that there'd be snow in November. Not my idea of a good time. But from 99 percent of his conversations lately, I've gotten the message that Tim is a real ski freak.

After supper I helped get things ready for Thanksgiving dinner. Aunt Carol, Uncle Peter, their two kids, my grandmother and my great grandmother were coming over the next day, all of them from out of town, and we always go all out to make everything really special for them.

I helped Mom make the crusts for two chocolate and three pumpkin pies. Two pies were for us and three were for a soup kitchen downtown, where my mom helps out once a week.

We worked side by side but hardly said a word to each other, except when Mom needed to give me instructions.

While Mom made cranberry sauce, I set the table. I love setting the table for company. First I spread our lace tablecloth and put out the good china dishes with the roses in the middle that used to belong to my father's parents, and put pink candles in our crystal candlesticks. Then I got out the sterling silverware that was given to my mother by her grandmother the night before my parents' wedding and that my mother has told us should be the third most important thing we rescue in case of a fire, besides ourselves, of course. The first is our picture albums and the second is a box of baby shoes, locks of hair, our old schoolwork, and other sentimental junk that Mom keeps in her closet. I laid a fork, spoon, and knife by each plate as straight and even as I could. I put a crystal water glass at every setting and a wine glass at the grown-ups' places.

My mother walked by and looked in just as I was folding the linen napkins to stand up on the plates, so I tried to look as if I wasn't enjoying myself.

I was still mad at her for calling my father home from work so they could gang up on me when I got home from school and one of them could jump in and take over when the other one got tired of lecturing me about the Never-Never Land caper. I'll bet it was worse than being interrogated by the police.

When Mom walked past the dining room that night, she just said, "I'm going to bed now. Turn out the lights when you come up." Then I knew she really felt bad. Usually she gushes and oohs and ahhs about how breathtakingly lovely the table looks. Then she picks up a piece of silverware and tells me it's a legacy and someday it'll belong to me.

I started to feel a little guilty.

I finished folding the napkins and walked slowly up the stairs. My parents' door was partly open. I

21

could see that they were sitting up in bed and Dad had a pile of papers on his lap while Mom was reading one of those kajillion-page paperbacks that you need a forklift to pick up.

I passed by their room, then turned around and went in. I stretched out on my stomach at the foot of their bed. Neither one looked up.

"Can I explain about today?" I said. They both put down what they were reading and looked at me. So I told them the whole story. I even told them how everyone thought we were on our way up the stairs but actually we were on our way down. Finally, I said I was sorry I embarrassed them.

"I'm glad you decided to come in here and I appreciate your apology, but I think we need to talk a little more about what happened, Patty," my mother said. "First of all, the fact that you embarrassed us isn't the main issue. I was embarrassed at first, but that was because when Sister Marianne called, she made me feel like I was thirteen again and standing in front of my principal, Sister Flaviana's desk twenty-five years ago. What you did was a lot more serious than just embarrassing your mother. You showed a lack of respect for other people." She was talking softly now, not yelling like she had earlier in the day. "You broke into someone's home, invaded his privacy, trespassed. Do you realize that?"

"I guess I didn't think of it that way."

"What if Father Damian or Sister Barbara Clare broke into our home and sneaked upstairs to look through your things?" Mom asked.

"I think they'd faint if they saw my room," I answered and laughed at the thought of Sister Clarabelle flipping her veil and running out of my room gagging.

"Be serious," Mom said.

"Sorry. I guess I just wasn't thinking."

"Well, from now on, think," Dad put in.

"I'm sorry. I really am," I said.

My father cleared his throat and went on, "The fact is, you embarrassed us, you broke rules, you broke the law. And the person you hurt the most was yourself. You . . ." I saw my mother's hand reach under the covers and hit Dad in the leg. He cleared his throat and said, "Apology accepted. Punishment still in effect."

My mother reached out and patted my back.

"I'll make it up to you, I promise," I said as I slid off the bed. "By the way, Mom, why were you getting chewed out by your principal when you were thirteen?"

"That's between me and Sister Flaviana and the fire department," Mom said with a grin.

Later, as I lay in bed, I wished I had never tried to sneak up to Father Damian's room.

3 The next morning I woke up to my mother shaking my shoulder.

"Happy Thanksgiving," she said cheerfully.

"That could have waited till I got up, Mom." I pulled the covers over my head.

She shook me again. "Patty, did you really mean it when you said you'd make it up to me?"

"Yeah," I said slowly. I was suddenly suspicious.

"Then would you come with me to St. Luke's Kitchen this morning?"

I pulled the covers off my head and sat up. "Aw, Mom. You know I don't like going there." I had gone with her once to St. Luke's, where they serve dinner every day to people who are poor or hungry and have no place else to go. Being there made me feel creepy and I decided I would never go back.

But now Mom was taking advantage. I jammed my feet into my bunny slippers and stomped to the bathroom. "Okay, I'll go, but only because I'm the kid and you're the parent and I have absolutely no rights."

Mom smiled. "That's my girl."

When we left at eleven o'clock, the turkey was in the oven and Dad was wearing his "Don't Complain To Me, I Just Work Here" apron and making French toast. Mary was sitting at the table in her booster chair whapping her plastic mug against the table and chanting "Cocoa Butts" over and over.

"Everything is under control," Dad told Mom. "Joel's in charge of potatoes, Chris is in charge of carrots, I'll handle the squash, and Mary is in charge of driving us all crazy. So go and don't worry about a thing." He saluted as we carried our pies out to the car.

At St. Luke's I sort of hung around the edges of the activity trying to look like I was doing something, while a bunch of people carved up a few turkeys and mashed a bunch of potatoes in enormous aluminum pots.

"Could you help set the tables?" Mom finally asked me. "Just put out napkins and silverware. The guests will get plates and cups in line."

Another kid about my age was there and followed me out to the dining room, carrying bins of silverware. He had on faded jeans with a tear above one knee that looked as if they had been through a war and lost, a plaid, flannel shirt, and well-worn leather sneakers that might in another lifetime have been white. He wore glasses, the wire-rimmed kind that I love on guys. On his head he wore a navy-blue baseball-style hat with the words "USS Parche" across the front.

"Your mom force you to come too?" I asked him.

"No. I come pretty often. I'm Alex."

"I'm Patty and I'm here against my will." He laughed and tossed a long package of paper napkins at me. I folded each one carelessly down the middle and slapped three pieces of unmatched silverware on top. As I worked I could see a line of people forming outside, young people and old, men and women. It gave me goosebumps to have them peering in the window at me, and I hoped none of them would try talking to me or shaking my hand or anything once they got inside. They all looked dirty, and I wished they'd had the consideration to wash up, at least on Thanksgiving.

They filed in and got plates of food and cups of coffee with real cream. I had to serve the mashed potatoes.

My mother was next to me serving gravy. She smiled and said "enjoy your dinner" to every single person. I was ready to scream by the time we were finished.

I was hoping we could leave after the last person got served, but my mother volunteered me to wash dishes. I was giving her a dirty look and making some excuse about the time, when Alex tossed a sponge at me and said, "You wash, I'll rinse."

We talked while I lathered up each dish and handed it to him. He said he was a sophomore at Jefferson High in the city and that he kind of liked coming to St. Luke's. I told him I went to St. Iggie's Junior High and I hated coming. Then I told him about the Never-Never Land caper and how it had gotten me cornered into coming to St. Luke's as a way of apologizing to my mother. He smiled a slow smile that started at the corners of his mouth and worked its way across his whole face. Then he broke into a big, rollicking laugh that made his eyes crinkle up. I started laughing too, and then flicked a handful of suds at him. It landed on his glasses. Before I knew it he had snapped his dish towel on my leg and I was chasing him around the kitchen with a sopping wet industrial-size sponge.

One of the adults yelled, "Hey, careful you two. The floor's slippery." So we went back to work. I took a few good looks at Alex as I handed him dishes. He was a little taller than me with blond, short hair and green eyes. He was sort of thin but it looked like there were muscles under his shirt. I decided he was okay.

When my mother told me it was time to go I was surprised to see that it was almost two o'clock already. I untied the huge white apron from around my waist and yanked it over my head. As we were leaving I jumped when I heard a voice call out, " 'Bye, Patty."

It was Alex. He was sitting at one of the tables talking to some men. One of them had a small whiskey bottle sticking up out of his pocket. It was disgusting.

I waved to Alex but didn't want to yell out " 'bye." I didn't want any of the men he was with to look up and think I was talking to them.

"Mother, why do you keep going there to feed those bums?" I asked when we were on our way home. "If those people didn't get free handouts, I bet they'd go get jobs fast."

"Please don't call them bums, Patty. You know, they're really not so different from you and me. They get happy, sad, lonely, scared, just like us. When I serve them I try to remember that each of them was once a child. Each of them, whether they're alcoholics or people with drug problems or emotional problems, or just plain poor, could have been a Patty or Joel or Chris or Mary, just like you kids. What's worse, maybe nobody ever loved them the way you kids are loved."

"Yeah, but no matter what happened to them, can't they just get jobs and start over?"

"It's not that easy. Did you notice the young man sitting near the door playing the harmonica?"

"Yeah, he kept bowing after every song, like he was in front of an audience."

"That's Rich. He's just a kid, really. He's tried to hold down job after job, but he can't handle it. He needs more help than just the hot meals we give him at St. Luke's."

"Well, I just want you to know that no matter how bad something hurt me I'd never let myself end up like those people. I have pride," I said.

"Oh, many of them have pride, too. Sometimes I want to tell them, 'It's okay. I don't pity you. I just want to help you a little, the same as I'd want someone to help me or my husband or kids if we ever needed it.'"

"Well, don't worry about me. I'll never need that kind of a handout," I repeated.

"A lot of them never thought they'd need a handout, either."

"How come most of them are men? I feel creepy around them."

"There are plenty of homeless women, even children and whole families. But St. Luke's is the oldest soup kitchen in Easton and it started out serving men so it stayed pretty much that way. If you went to St. Martin's Kitchen you'd see lots of women and children."

"You're not going to make me go to St. Martin's, are you?"

"Don't worry. I won't make you go to St. Martin's or even St. Luke's anymore."

We drove in silence for a while. "By the way, what's the story on Alex?" I asked, as we pulled in our driveway.

"He's the son of a lawyer, Tom Henley, who works as an advocate for the poor. I think some of his work involves giving legal aid to migrant farm workers. Alex comes with his dad to St. Luke's quite often. The men like it when he comes because he plays chess with them."

"Yeah, like they know how to play chess. *I* don't even know how to play chess."

Mom didn't answer. She just smiled in a way that really frosted me.

The rest of the day went fine, and that night, I

wrote a lot in my notebook. Whenever it's a holiday I like to write all about it, because it's sort of history.

I described what we ate and how my mom and all the other women relatives did their annual "correcting of the stuffing recipe." I wrote about how the men watched the football game on TV and about the pink streak my cousin Nancy dyed in her hair. She told me her mom (my aunt Carol) practically fainted when she saw it and didn't want to come to Thanksgiving just because of what the relatives would think. I told Nancy about the Never-Never Land caper and how my mom was the same way.

Nancy dared me to dye a pink streak in my hair. I wondered if Tim would like me better that way.

I closed my notebook and put it back in its hiding place on my bookshelf behind the gold-lettered set of *The World's Greatest Classics*, which my parents gave me for Christmas when I was eleven, and which I have not yet started to read, but I will.

I got into bed but I couldn't sleep. After a few minutes I got up and pulled out my notebook again. I wrote:

Today I helped Mom at St. Luke's Kitchen. I hated it. I was sort of scared of the people there, but mostly I was mad.

I was scared they might yell at me or start a fight or something if they didn't like the food.

And I was mad at them for being bums and making people like Mom feel bad for them. I mean, why do they want to live like that anyway? Why don't they just clean up and get jobs so there wouldn't have to be soup kitchens and I wouldn't have to see them all dirty?

Mom says they can't help it but I don't believe her. I have problems and I still wash my hair every single day.

I closed the notebook and got back into bed, but I still couldn't sleep. I kept hearing sad harmonica music inside my head.

Friday, Saturday, and Sunday dragged till I thought I'd go nuts. Joel and Chris were busy doing things with their friends, so I was the only one around for Mary to annoy. She bugged me about every five minutes to play "Hungry, Hungry Hippos" with her. I could stand the game for the first kajillion times but after that it started to get on my nerves. Do you know how hard it is to let a kid win just about every game for three solid days? My father says we shouldn't always let her win, but we do. After a while I wondered how many games it would take before she realized that I never won, and would feel sorry for me. But right up to Sunday night, after every game Miss Greedy would sit on the floor and laugh till she toppled over.

By bedtime Sunday I had given my hair a hot oil treatment, polished my fingernails and toenails, experimented with my mother's mascara, alphabetized my cassette tapes, untangled all my jewelry, read three scenes ahead of where we're supposed to be in *Romeo and Juliet,* and almost, I repeat almost, started to clean up my room.

I had also bribed Joel by promising to do his turn at kitchen clean-up three times if he would call Tracy for me and ask her how it was going at her house. He did, only to find out that Tracy wasn't allowed to talk on the phone either. Then he had the nerve to hold me to my promise anyway.

Let me go on record as saying that I have never looked forward to Monday as much as I did that weekend.

4 Tracy and I ride the same bus. In fact, she lives in a house right across the road from the Easton College campus, where I live in housing reserved for faculty, so we even have the same bus stop.

On Monday morning I ran as fast as I could through the brown, crackly leaves that covered the campus like a blanket. I couldn't wait to see Tracy. The two of us spent the entire thirty-minute ride into the city comparing punishments.

I found out that besides grounding her for a week, Tracy's parents had made her write a letter of apology to Father John and Sister Marianne. I hoped my parents wouldn't get wind of that method of torture.

Of course the news about our attempted invasion of Never-Never Land was all over school and we got bombarded with attention. Everybody was treating us like celebrities but I wasn't feeling like one. After what my parents had said about trespassing and people's privacy and stuff, I wasn't very proud of myself. I wished everyone would just drop the whole thing, especially in homeroom, where Sister Clarabelle stood near her desk listening to every word.

At lunch everyone at our table jumped on us with questions about it, everyone being: Jeannie

Croydon, a super-brain I got to know from working on the school newspaper with her; Allison Jewett, who was on the field hockey team with Tracy last year; Trish Hoffman, a girl I met in the school play this fall; Kate Donnelly, my second-best friend from elementary school; and Whitney Wixsome, who is gorgeous and poised and makes me feel like a bigger gawk than ever when I'm around her. She's the kind of girl you want to hate because of her looks, but she's so nice you have to like her.

Tracy finally hit the table with her spoon, like a judge gaveling for order, to get everyone to shut up. When they did, she said quietly, "I'll tell you the story once and then Patty and I don't want to talk about it any more. We went to Father Damian's room, took a couple of pictures, got caught, and got two weeks detention. The end. Let's eat."

"Sure," Trish Hoffman said. "The way I heard the story you never made it up there."

"Yeah," piped in Allison. "I'll believe it when I see the pictures."

"In that case you'll never believe it because the film got ruined," Tracy said simply.

"Oh, how handy," Allison answered kind of sarcastically.

The more everyone talked about it, the dumber I felt. If we had pulled it off we would have scored a perfect ten on the coolness scale. But we had gotten caught. And we had ruined the evidence. Definitely not cool. I was glad Tracy had told everyone we didn't want to talk about it anymore.

The conversation turned to Thanksgiving and we talked for a few minutes about vacation. Since I had done absolutely nothing, I talked about how much I missed Tim. It's funny, whenever I talk about Tim I have everyone's attention. Nobody breaks in to say things like, "Hey, anybody want to trade sandwiches?" or stuff like that. It makes me feel kind of important.

Whitney was the first one at our table to have a boyfriend, I was the second, and since two weeks ago Tracy's been going out with Tim's friend, Scott, so she's the third. But I was second, can you believe it? Me.

After a few minutes of not talking about the Never-Never Land caper, Kate finally blurted out, "I know the subject is supposed to be closed, but I just have to ask you Patty. Why didn't you use the 'twenty-four-hour rule' on Tracy when she came up with such a nutty idea? I mean, you two really went overboard this time."

We have four rules at our lunch table:

1. News, information, or discussion of anything relating to the opposite sex has top priority.

2. No one is allowed to ask what anybody else got on a test.

3. If Kate brings one of her onion sandwiches she has to sit somewhere else.

4. When Tracy tries to get us involved in one of her "super ideas" we call the twenty-four-hour rule on her. That means we can order her to stop talking about it for one day, during which time we can think it over and realize that it is dumb and crazy.

Tracy is usually the one who gets us into trouble. She has a gift for making the most bogus ideas sound great. One time in third grade she convinced me it would look cute to ink X's in all the pale gray squares on my plaid school uniform. I went right to work and got halfway around the skirt before my teacher saw it. She didn't think it was so cute. My parents didn't think it was cute, either, and they made me pay half the cost of a new uniform out of my allowance.

It's this kind of thing that made us devise the twenty-four-hour rule for Tracy. But I didn't want to admit to the girls that the reason I hadn't used it in connection with the Never-Never Land caper was because it had started out being my idea.

I was saved from answering Kate by the end-of-lunch bell ringing. As Tracy wadded up her waxed paper and stuffed it into her lunch bag, she said she'd meet me at my locker after school and we'd go to detention together. She called it detention club and asked me if I thought we could list it as an activity after our name in the yearbook.

"You're a real yahoo," I said.

"It'll be fun." Tracy punched me in the arm and stood up to leave.

"Why don't you take pictures of detention so we'll know you really went," Allison said. "And try not to let the film get ruined this time."

Tracy hit her over the head with her lunch bag as she passed behind her seat. "Why don't you have pictures taken of your brain so we'll know you have one?"

"Take notes," Kate called out as Tracy and I walked away, "in case any of us ever gets detention. And be sure you don't sit in anyone's reserved seat."

"Teach us any new words you learn from the scum balls down there," Trish added.

"Everything will be fine," Whitney said, looking worried. "The kids in detention are probably very nice, just like you."

"I'd wear a bag over my head if I were you," Jeannie offered.

Tracy was wrong. Detention wasn't fun. It was terrifying. When we stood in front of room B-17 after eighth period I started shaking so hard Tracy put her arm around my shoulder and said, "Hey, don't worry. I'm with you."

"Oh, that makes me feel a lot better," I answered sarcastically. I didn't care if the Pope was with me, I didn't want to walk into that room and give my name and have all the sub-human forms of life in the detention room look at me and smirk.

Real losers get detention, the fast crowd of kids who get picked up in the parking lot after school by older kids wearing denim jackets with skulls painted on them. Nice kids don't get detention, and up till that day, I had thought of myself as one of the nice kids.

During detention Tracy risked getting in even more trouble by passing me a note:

Dear Club Member,

What do you think of detention so far? What do you think of all these jerks in here? What do you think they think of you? How come the detention teacher doesn't smile? How come no one in here smiles? How come you're not smiling? What is there to smile about? Why does it feel like we've been here for three hours? Why is the teacher staring at me? If she comes near me should I eat this note? Why am I asking all these questions? Why are you reading all these questions? Do you need psychiatric help? Do I need psychiatric help? Does the detention teacher need psychiatric help? Is the detention teacher a former psychiatric patient? Why do I feel like bursting out laughing? Why can't I stop asking questions? Why did someone write "your mama" on the top of this desk? How am I going to get this note to you? Why are you staring at your fingernails? Why am I staring at your fingernails? Why is the girl next to you cleaning her fingernails with a switchblade?

From,
Me

That night Tim called, and my heart started to pound the minute I heard his voice. I hadn't talked to him since the episode on Wednesday when Joel yanked the phone out of my hand right after I said "hello."

Tim said he missed me while he was away and told me that I was the talk of St. Iggie's, at least the east side of St. Iggie's. I told him I was the talk of the west side that day, too. He laughed, and I sighed with relief.

I was ready to tell him about the weird kids in the detention room when he changed the subject and proceeded to spend half an hour talking about skiing. At first I kept myself from going bonkers by biting my nails. Then Chris wandered into the hall and went running out yelling, "Mom! Patty's biting her nails!" So I quit that and just flipped through a magazine while he talked. Luckily Dad walked by and pointed to his watch so I told Tim my father wanted me to get off the phone.

I hung up and took the phone into the closet to call Tracy.

"Trace," I said, "I've got a problem."

"If it has anything to do with tomorrow's quiz on *Romeo and Juliet*, save your breath."

"Worse. It's about Tim. I feel like he's losing interest in me. All he cares about is his dumb skiing. All he talks about is his dumb skiing. Did you ever see him on those dumb skis with the roller-skate wheels on the bottom? He trains on them for two hours every single day so he'll make the dumb ski team."

"Yeah, Scott's the same way."

"Doesn't it bother you?"

"Hey, I've only known Scott for two weeks. And the second week I spent grounded. It's not like we're a hot item or anything."

"Well, it bothers me a lot. When we first met, Tim used to try to think of interesting things to talk about and he used to be interested in what I had to say. Now he doesn't care if he bores the socks off me."

"Well, if that's how it is, maybe you'd be better off without Tim. You could beg Gary Holmes to take you back."

"I'm trying to talk seriously here for a minute, if you don't mind, Tracy Gilmore. And I'd appreciate it if you wouldn't use the words Gary Holmes in the same breath with the words Tim Shokow."

"Sorry. I lost my head there for a minute."

I lowered my voice, even though I had the closet door shut. "Tracy, the thing is, I love Tim."

"You what?" Tracy asked in a whisper.

"I love Tim."

"How do you know?"

"I just know. Take my word for it."

"When did this happen?"

"I don't know. I didn't check my watch, for Pete's sake. It just happened."

Joel chose that moment to start yanking at the phone cord under the door. I was afraid he'd hear if I said any more, so Tracy and I hung up.

I went upstairs and lay down on my bed. I thought about Tracy's question and tried to think back to when I had first realized I loved Tim. Maybe it happened riding the late bus together when he stayed after school for football and I stayed for play rehearsals. If it weren't for the late bus that takes a long route through half the county to drive kids home, we wouldn't have had much chance to be together. We live miles apart. Tim's in the city and I'm in the suburbs.

I got out my diary and drew a school bus in it. Then I wrote the words for the first time.

November 28

♡♡ I L♡VE TIM SH♡K♡W ♡ ♡

How I know it's love :

1. *I think about him constantly.*
2. *When he calls me on the phone, my heart pounds like crazy.*
3. *When he touches me I get goose bumps*

4. When he's near me my legs turn to jello
5. My hands sweat when we're together
6.
7.
8.
9.
10.

I decided to lie down in bed while I tried to think of more reasons, but I guess I fell asleep because the next thing I knew, it was morning and Mary was sitting on my stomach scribbling with black marker all over my notebook. You couldn't even read where I had written

♡♡ I L♡VE TIM SH♡K♡W ♡♡

Tuesday at lunch I was forced to use the twenty-four-hour rule on Tracy. As soon as we sat down she announced, between bites of a bologna and mustard sandwich, "Patty, I have a super idea. You are going to take up skiing. It's the only way."

"The only way to what?" I asked. "Break all the major bones in my body? Forget it."

"It's the only way to keep Tim interested in you," Tracy explained calmly. "Look, you said yourself that he's supposed to be your boyfriend, but all he does is talk about skiing, go roller-skate skiing and plan for a winter of skiing."

"Yeah, well all I'm planning is to stay in one piece at least to the end of eighth grade. I have a genetic weakness called 'chicken-itis.' The main symptom is fear of sailing down a hill at one hundred miles an hour on two wooden sticks. No thanks and I hereby call the twenty-four-hour rule on you so let's change the subject."

"Okay, but you know what they say," she answered as she flattened her milk carton, flipped her braid over her shoulder and got up to leave.

"No," I called after her, "I don't know what they say." She kept walking. "What do they say?" I yelled.

But Tracy was almost out of the cafeteria and the teacher who was cafeteria monitor that day was closing in on me hissing "Shhhhh" and asking me my name and homeroom.

Tracy didn't say a word about skiing for the rest of the day. Tim did, though, when he called that night. I took the phone into the hall closet for privacy and was all ready to give him an update on the day's new members in the detention club, when he started talking about bindings and moguls and stem christies till I wanted to scream. So I did. Of course I was sorry the instant I did it, but the scream had already started before my brain kicked in to inform me that I was doing something majorly stupid.

"I'm sorry. I'm sorry," I said, getting all nervous. "Tim? Are you there? Do you forgive me?"

43

"You nearly busted my eardrum," Tim said after a few seconds. "What was that all about?"

"It's just that all you talk about is skiing. You talk about it so much it makes me want to scream."

"So you did. That's my Patty. Okay, I get the hint. Well, I'd like to talk about something else, but it sounds like someone is ringing church bells inside my head. I'd better hang up and get over to Emergency and have my eardrum replaced."

I was hoping that before he hung up he'd say something about us going out over the weekend or even mention that he'd stop over some night to see me. But he didn't.

"I'm sorry about the scream," I apologized again. "If you want to stop over after school some day, I could make it up to you by baking you some brownies."

"Don't worry about it, really. Well, gotta go."

"Yeah, me too. 'Bye."

My face felt very hot all of a sudden. I hung up and kicked the closet door.

At lunch the next day I was in the middle of telling how Sister Clarabelle had called me up to her desk that morning to tell me what a shame it was I had besmudged my record at St. Ignatius by taking part in an unbecoming act of impropriety, when Tracy looked at her watch and cut in, picking up her train of thought from exactly twenty-four hours ago.

"What people say is that if it's worth keeping, it's worth fighting for, Patty. If you think Tim is worth fighting for, go into combat armed with ski poles and lift tickets. We can take the lessons together, if you want. The only reason I haven't learned up till now is that you keep talking me out of it. But I think the time has come." She laid a ski brochure on top of my peanut butter and jelly sandwich.

"Skiing's awesome!" Allison put in, as she peeled a banana. "You'd love it, Patty—the wind in your face, the sense of incredible speed, the control over your body, the challenge of . . ."

"Cool it," Tracy said, blowing the paper off her straw at Allison's face. "You're not helping, believe me."

Tracy turned back to me and continued, "I checked at the Recreation Center and they're offering ski classes. One indoor lesson and two outdoor, for beginners. What do you say? Just give it a try."

"Trace, you know I'm not heavily into physical exertion. Anything more demanding than getting my jeans zipped is out of my league."

"Do you love Tim or don't you?" she asked under her breath.

"Oh, for Pete's sake, I'll think about taking lessons," I said. And that was enough for Tracy.

When I walked into sixth-period English class she was sitting in the seat nearest the door. She held up one foot under the front of the desk, showing the sole of her shoe. On it was inked: Ski Your

Way. Then she lifted her other foot, leaning back in her chair so I got a good look at the sole: Into His Heart.

I shook my head and smiled, just as Tracy lost her balance and fell over backward, chair and all.

Every day for the rest of the week I baked brownies the minute I got home from detention club. But Tim never came to collect. In fact, he didn't even call. I felt like there was an empty chunk in my life.

5 Joel and I were spending Saturday morning the way we always do, sleeping till ten, then having a leisurely breakfast of cold, leftover pizza. I sat at the kitchen table with my hair uncombed, wearing my nightshirt with the rip in one shoulder, munching on a piece of pepperoni as I read the funnies. Joel was across from me skimming the Teenspeak page of the newspaper while he gnawed on a rock-hard crust.

"Hey," he said, "this letter in the advice column sounds like you wrote it. Listen." Joel folded the paper and laid it on the table, then read: "Dear Dr. Jamesworth: My brother and I are a year apart. He is smarter, better looking, and more popular than I am. It's making me miserable. What can I do? Signed, Miss Inferiority Complex."

"Get real, Joel. In your dreams I wrote that letter," I said. "So, what is the all-knowing psychologist's advice?"

"Let's see. He says that all brothers and sisters who are close in age compare themselves to each other and Inferiority Complex is so busy watching her brother she isn't bothering to take a good look at her own strong points. He tells her to make a list of five faults and five virtues in her brother and five faults and virtues in herself. Then she's supposed to talk to her brother about it."

"In your case it can't be done. You don't have five virtues," I said and went to the fridge for a glass of orange juice.

"Yeah, I only have one, perfection." Joel got up and left the room before I could think of a smart answer.

As I was prying my third piece of pizza out of the box, the doorbell rang. Chris came thundering down the stairs to answer it. Mary was hot at his heels yelling, "Me do it! Me do it!" By the time Chris beat her to the door she was crying so hysterically I couldn't hear who our visitor was. I hoped it wasn't Tracy with some new bit of ammunition to use in her battle to get me to take skiing lessons.

My pizza dropped from my hand when I heard the words, "Is Patty home?" coming from the mouth of Tim Shokow.

"Yeah, come on in," answered Chris. Then he proceeded to call me at the top of his lungs as he went back upstairs, leaving Tim standing in the hall.

I was trapped. There was no way I could face Tim looking like a bag lady, but I couldn't get to my room to make myself presentable with Tim blocking the stairway. I ducked into the little powder room off the kitchen, that Dad had converted from a pantry years ago. I brushed my teeth, combed my hair and washed the pizza sauce off my chin, then stood there with the door closed hoping someone would come to my rescue. No one did and after a few minutes Chris yelled down the stairs to Tim, "Maybe she's in the kitchen."

I heard Tim walk into the kitchen and sit down at the table. I waited, breathing in slow motion so he wouldn't hear. I heard Tim turning pages of the newspaper. Still I waited, not moving a muscle and hoping I wasn't standing on the floorboard that sometimes creaks. I could hear the minutes ticking away on the big school clock in the front hall. Sweat was running down my sides. It didn't take me long to realize that nothing was going to save me.

My father's faded brown terry robe happened to be lying on the wicker clothes hamper so I put it on and wrapped the big tie around my waist. It looked even rattier on me than it does on him, but luckily it was so long it dragged on the floor, covering up the unmatched socks I had worn to bed the night before. I threw my shoulders back and opened the door.

"Hi, Tim. Sorry to keep you waiting," I smiled as I shut the door quickly behind me.

Tim looked like he wanted to evaporate into thin air. His face got all red and he stammered, looking down at his feet, "Maybe I should have called first, but I was just out training so I thought I'd roller ski over to your house to say hi."

"No problem, just give me a minute. I'll be right down," I said as I attempted to glide gracefully out of the room. I had taken three steps when I abruptly got yanked backward by the tie on my father's robe, which was caught in the powder-room door. I pulled the tie free, glided out of the room, then raced up the stairs two at a time.

First I went to Chris's room. I stuck my head in and growled, "You, mister, are dead meat." I slammed the door and ran for my room, throwing the robe off as I went. You would not believe a human being could put on makeup, get dressed and do her hair as fast as I did it that morning. Within minutes I was back in the kitchen, graciously offering Tim a piece of pizza.

He refused. "I was expecting brownies," he said.

"I could make you some," I volunteered and self-consciously started rooting through the bowl cupboard for the big mixing bowl.

"No, just kidding," Tim laughed. "I just stopped by for a minute. Scott is outside. We've got to hit the road."

As we walked to the front door Tim asked what was new and how the family was. He apologized for not calling as often as he'd like but explained that he was busy training so he'd make the school ski team. I apologized again for screaming in his ear on the phone. Then he just walked out with a wave of his hand. He never said a word about seeing me that night or the next day, or about calling me. Nothing. Just, " 'Bye, Patty." Scott called out "hi" from where he was sitting on the bottom front step and they both pushed off on their skis-on-wheels.

I watched the back of Tim's curly head and his broad shoulders move farther and farther away from me. I went into the house and called Tracy.

"I'll take the ski lessons," I said. "Come over after lunch and we can bike to the Rec Center to sign up. Now you'd better hang up and go get dressed. I have a feeling your doorbell is about to ring."

I went to my room and pulled out my diary. I wrote:

MY FAULTS   MY VIRTUES
_____   _____

1.   1.

2.   2.
3.   3.

4.   4.

5.   5.

I thought for a long time before I finally got all the spaces filled in. Then I did the same for Joel. When I finished my lists looked like this:

MY FAULTS

1. Mock people out, especially when I'm with my friends.
2. Complain too much.
3. Not nice to Chris, even though he's a creep.
4. Keep my feelings inside
5. Not enough self-confidence
6. Don't think before I act
7. Bite my nails

MY VIRTUES

1. Honesty
2. Sense of humor
3. People can count on me
4. Love my parents
5. ~~Good writer Loyal~~
5. Have Tim for a boyfriend

JOEL'S FAULTS

1. ~~Thinks he's perfect~~
1. Acts like he's older than me
2. Gets better grades than me
3. Too private
4. Doesn't pay enough attention to clothes
5.

JOEL'S VIRTUES

1. Self confidence
2. Likes himself
3. Organized
4. Smart
5. Easy to talk to
6. Doesn't tell when he knows something I did wrong.

I put the diary back in its hiding place on my bookshelf. I decided I would show the lists to Joel and talk about them someday soon.

The next order of business was to find Chris and pulverize him. I searched the house but he had made himself invisible.

"Where's that little worm?" I asked my mother.

"What little worm?" she asked innocently.

"The little worm who is out to destroy my life; the little worm who invites boys into the kitchen when I'm sitting in there with pepperoni breath and Tina Turner hair."

"If you mean Chris, he made sudden plans to sleep at Tiger Borkman's house. Now I understand why he called the sleepover a matter of life and death."

That afternoon I found myself sitting at a folding table in the front hall of the Rec Center, writing "Patricia Dillman" on a registration form for ski lessons. Tracy was totally hyper.

"Finally, I'm going to ski!" she kept saying.

When Tracy and I handed in our forms along with fifteen dollars, Tracy noticed some pamphlets stacked on the counter.

"Hey, there's a ski trip to Benton during Christmas vacation!" she said beaming, and took four of the pale green advertising flyers. "One for you, one for me, and two to slip through the air vents of Scott's and Tim's lockers," she explained.

Benton is Benton Mountain Ski Resort, a two-hour drive from Easton. Since we have about five months of snow around here, lots of people ski, and Benton is where they all go. But I've never had any urge to meet the mountain face to face.

As we walked out into the cold December air, she punched me in the arm and smiled. "You're a good egg, you know that, Pats?" she said.

"I only hope I don't end up getting scrambled," I answered, and rubbed the spot where she had belted me.

"I don't think we should tell the guys," Tracy said as we unlocked our bikes. "Let's surprise them by showing up on the slopes after we've mastered the basics."

When I got home the first thing I did was take the phone into the hall closet and call Tim to tell him about the lessons.

"Awesome!" he said. "Hey, could I come over right now and give you a pre-first-lesson lesson? Then you can face out everyone in your class."

"But I don't even own skis!" I had to laugh at how excited he was.

"Not to worry," he said. "Most of skiing is done with the mind and body and I can teach you how to control them before you ever tighten a binding."

"Can you hold on a minute?" I asked. I ran to check the blackboard that hangs near the side door of our old Victorian house. Every single day my mother lists a job for each of us kids. No matter how busy she is, she never forgets to list a job. I was hoping it would be a small job that day or some kind of a job I could fake. But, no. On the blackboard, under "Patty," were two messages: "Patty has cooties" written in Chris's sloppy handwriting, and "Help Dad clean the garage—3 till 5 P.M."

I came back to the phone and apologized, "Sorry, but I have some jobs to do around the house this afternoon. How about tonight?"

"Great! I have this book, *Anyone Can Ski* that I could lend you. How about seven-thirty?"

"Okay, tonight, seven-thirty," I agreed.

"We are going to have so much fun this winter!" Tim boomed into the phone as he hung up.

I carried the phone out of the closet, thinking about the interesting turn of events. All of a sudden Mr. Busy had time for me. All of a sudden, the minute he found out I was taking skiing lessons, he could have one of his parents drive him all the way to my house, spend time with me, and then have someone come back to pick him up, all without disturbing his precious training schedule.

I decided I wasn't going to do him the honor of falling all over him. I wouldn't even change my clothes. After supper I sat at my desk wearing the sweatshirt and sweatpants I had worn to clean the garage, trying to concentrate on how covalent bonding of atoms works. Instead, I couldn't help lecturing myself on my future attitude toward Tim.

I decided that from now on, my world was not going to revolve around Tim Shokow. There were other things in life. Sure, I loved him but I wasn't going to worship the ground he walked on.

As I was lecturing myself, the doorbell rang and my body went instantly weak all over. I jumped out of my chair, knocking my science book to the floor, and yanked open a dresser drawer. I started pulling sweaters out and tossing them on the bed one by one. I pulled off my sweatshirt, sprayed on some deodorant and put on my nubby peach sweater. I stripped off my sweatpants and replaced them with a pair of frosted jeans. I brushed my hair furiously, put on some lipstick and Face-Glo. Then I took a deep breath and walked slowly and nonchalantly down the stairs.

The hall was empty. I opened the front door and peered out into the darkness. Just then Chris pushed past me, running out the door.

"Forgot my He-man figures," he yelled, and jumped into the Borkmans' car, clutching a shoe-box under his arm.

For sure, that kid was dead meat. I went back upstairs and tried on five more outfits before the doorbell rang again. This time it was Tim, fifteen minutes late.

I was planning on being mad but the first thing he said was, "You look great in red." Of course I turned to mush and forgave him.

"You mean you don't like me in gray and blue plaid, with a white blouse and white knee socks and brown tie shoes that look like they could survive a nuclear explosion?" I asked as we walked into the den.

"That's a close second. And I bet my third favorite thing on you is going to be skis," he said as he sat down on the red imitation leather couch and opened his ski book in his lap.

"Yeah, right," I answered dully and sat down next to him. He inched closer to me and spread the book open on both our laps. The sides of our arms were touching and every time he turned a page his arm rubbed against mine and sent a shiver through me. Once in a while he'd reach over to point to some diagram he was explaining and his breath would feel warm against my face. I could not concentrate.

He went through the first three chapters, and I never heard a word he said. I was busy studying his big, square hands and glancing, every time I dared, at the way his hair curled up at the back of his neck, over the edge of his shirt collar.

"Got it so far?" Tim asked.

"Yeah, right," I answered.

"Okay. Stand up and show me."

What? Show him what? I had no idea what I was supposed to show him. I stood up slowly. "Hey, I have an idea. Why don't we take a break first and I'll show you a glass of Pepsi and a bowl of tortilla chips."

We heard a car horn in the driveway. Tim looked at his watch. "Omigosh, I've been here an hour and a half! That must be my dad." He closed the book and grabbed his jacket.

"Did I help you, even a little?" he asked as we walked toward the hall.

"Oh yes, definitely. Definitely, yes. This was so awesomely helpful to me. I feel like I could go out and ski down a mountain right now. And I'm sorry your dad came already, just when I was going to demonstrate that thing for you."

"Well, next time. Next time I come we'll start with a demonstration by future Olympic gold medalist Patty, the Hot Dog, Dillman."

"Should I be flattered or insulted that you just called me a hot dog?"

"Definitely flattered. A hot dog is somebody who does awesome tricks on skis."

"Yeah, right."

Tim called out " 'bye" to my mom and dad in the kitchen and then took both my hands in his. He squeezed them as he said, "This was great. Now you be sure to memorize that book and I'll give you lesson number two in a few days."

As Tim walked out the door we saw that a few snowflakes had started to fall. Tim gave the thumbs up sign as he headed to his car.

"Yeah, right," I mumbled to myself as I shut the door.

I took the phone into the closet and dialed Tracy.

"Look," I apologized, "I know you told me not

to tell Tim about the ski lessons, but we were talking on the phone this afternoon and he somehow wormed it out of me. Sorry."

"That's okay. In fact the same thing happened to me. I was talking to Scott and it slipped out."

"I guess that means we can't back out gracefully."

"Since when have we ever done anything gracefully, anyway?"

"Yeah, right."

We hung up and I went into the den. I flipped through the pages of *Anyone Can Ski* trying to figure out what I was supposed to demonstrate.

6 One of the reasons no one wants Sister Clarabelle for homeroom is that she schedules a conference with each of her students. She takes them into this little storage room in the back of her homeroom and talks about Life. She expects the student to pour her heart out and tell all her feelings and problems and junk like that.

When I walked into homeroom on Monday morning I groaned when I saw my name chalked in the corner of the front blackboard under the words:

This Week's Conference

written in Sister Clarabelle's flowery script. The only good thing about the conference was that I'd get out of detention for that day.

Later, when I came back to Clarabelle's room for religion class, all I could do was stare at my name on the board and bite my nails, wondering if she has some way of hypnotizing kids to make them confess all the bad things they've ever done.

I was planning how I'd keep my eyes down the whole conference and mumble all my answers, when I heard my name called. "Patricia, what have you selected as your project?" It was Sister Clarabelle, and I had no idea what she was talking about.

Helen Zelczak, who sits behind me, leaned forward and whispered into my hair, "She wants to know what you picked for your corporal work of mercy project."

I groaned. I could recite the works of mercy in one breath, blindfolded, standing on my head, underwater, and explain that they were ways of showing that we care for other people by helping them with their needs, but I had forgotten all about the project. And Sister Clarabelle was staring at me saying, "Now that Helen has refreshed your memory, could you please share with the class the nature of your project?"

Boy, I wished she would speak in normal earth talk and also cut out the sarcasm.

I stood up slowly, taking time to pull up my regulation knee socks and tuck in my blouse, while I groped through my brain for something to say. All of a sudden, my mother's words came back to me and I said, "My project is to volunteer my time once a week at St. Luke's Kitchen, serving meals to the men and women who walk the streets hungry because life has dealt them some bad blows, and who need our help, not our pity."

Sister Clarabelle stared at me for a minute. Then she flipped her little veil over her shoulder and said, "Thank you, Patricia. That is a beautiful project and well expressed. I look forward to your written report at the end of the semester." The bell rang and we all scrambled for the door.

I walked out of the room loaded with guilt about

being so phony. But when I'm eyeball to eyeball with the wrath of Clarabelle, I become capable of stooping so low my tongue drags on the floor.

"I think she hates me," I told everyone at lunch that day, "and when I go into that storeroom for my conference tomorrow, if I'm not out in half an hour, break down the door."

Tracy had laughed and said, "No sweat. Just remember two rules. One: Don't volunteer information. Just answer, 'yes, Sister' or, 'no, Sister' to everything. And, two: Under no circumstances are you to mention my name."

"Don't worry," added Whitney, "you're so nice, no one could possibly hate you, not even Clarabelle."

I thanked Whitney for the compliment, but the truth is, she thinks everyone's nice. She even calls Gary Holmes a "cool dude."

On the day of the conference, as I stood at the girls' room mirror trying to wipe off my lipstick just to be on the safe side, Tracy gave me a Hershey's Kiss, which is kind of a tradition with us. We always give each other Hershey's Kisses as a sign of support.

When I walked into the storeroom Sister Clarabelle was sitting at a little table facing the door. She motioned toward a chair across from her. I looked around to make sure she didn't have a tape recorder hidden, then sat down and pulled my skirt over my knees. I tried to believe what Whitney had said at lunch.

Sister Clarabelle folded her hands on the table and said, "First of all, Patricia, I want to tell you that everything we say here is strictly confidential. It will never go beyond these walls."

"Yes, Sister."

"Are you nervous?"

"Yes, Sister."

"There's no reason to be. The rumors you've heard about mean old Sister Clarabelle are greatly exaggerated."

My face turned red.

"How is eighth grade going for you so far, Patricia?"

"Fine, Sister, except for detention."

"Ah, yes, detention. You know, I don't believe in detention. I believe punishment should be a positive rather than a negative form of corrective discipline. If I had been in charge you and Tracy would be scraping lunch trays or some such job."

"Yes, Sister." I mentally thanked God Sister Clarabelle wasn't in charge.

"Have you learned anything from the experience?"

"Yes, Sister." There was a long pause. I crossed my knees, then uncrossed them and crossed my ankles instead, which Sister Clarabelle says is more ladylike. Finally she spoke.

"I was hoping you might elaborate on that 'yes, Sister.'"

"Yes, Sister. What I learned was that I should have more respect for people's privacy and that sometimes the things we do hurt other people. My mother really took it personally and totally spazzed out."

"I'm glad to hear that," Sister Clarabelle said. Then she blushed and got all flustered. "What I mean is that I'm glad you learned something. I'm not glad your mother, as you put it, totally spazzed out. Patricia, I realize you are a young lady with a highly active imagination. Someday that will serve you well. As Albert Einstein once said, 'Imagination is more important than knowledge.' But for now, I'm afraid your imagination serves to involve you in troublesome situations. As of this moment, though, let's put the whole episode of your visit to the third floor behind us. Agreed?"

"Yes, Sister."

"Let's talk instead about your family. Do you have any brothers or sisters?"

"Yes, Sister. I have two brothers and a sister, all younger than me."

Sister Clarabelle leaned forward. "It's difficult to be the oldest, isn't it? I was the oldest of eight children, and I disliked it intensely. I felt I was given too much responsibility."

"Yeah, me too. And whenever I'm in charge no one listens to me. They goof off and I get the blame. It stinks. Excuse me, Sister, I mean it isn't fair."

"Sometimes life can seem very unfair. But, you know something, Patricia? I think you have a good

64

head on your shoulders. Despite your antics, at the core of your being, you are a sensible person. Now tell me, do you have any career aspirations?"

"Does that mean what do I want to be when I grow up?"

She nodded her head and smiled so I went on, "I want to be a journalist. I love to write. I want to travel all over the world and meet famous people and someday I want to write a book about them. I try to write in my diary every day. I write whatever comes into my head without worrying that other people will read it and think I'm wacko. And I love writing my opinion column for the school paper," I rambled on. Suddenly I caught myself. I settled back in my chair and shut up.

"You will never guess what I wanted to be," Sister Clarabelle said in a low voice, leaning forward. "I wanted to be an artist. After I graduated from high school I worked in a department store during the day and took art lessons at night. It took me a year before I realized that I didn't have very much talent. My teacher was leading me on, just to make money. Sometimes people are not what they seem to be."

"Yeah, like my boyfriend Tim. Lately I think he only pays attention to me when he feels like it. I wish I knew how to make things like they were when we first met." As soon as the words came out of my mouth I mentally gave myself a swift kick for mentioning Tim. When I get nervous I tend to ramble. I reminded myself to limit my answers to "yes, Sister" and "no, Sister."

"You're young, Patricia. For the next few years boys will come into your life and they will go out of your life. Sometimes they will lose interest in you and sometimes you will lose interest in them. It's part of growing up. And, Patricia, what I'm going to say will sound like nun talk, but listen anyway. At your age life is full of wonderful things. It shouldn't center on boys. Put some of your energies into schoolwork and writing and girlfriends and your family. Put everything in perspective."

"Yes, Sister." I didn't dare tell Sister it wouldn't work; that I think about Tim a jillion times a day. I didn't dare tell her about how I love Tim and how my heart pounds every time I see him.

Sister Clarabelle smiled. She asked me about my school subjects and lots of other stuff. After a while she happened to glance down at her watch. "My goodness, our time is up. Thank you for sharing your thoughts with me, Patricia. Good luck with your writing and with your project at St. Luke's soup kitchen."

"Sister, could I ask you one question?"

"Of course, my dear."

"When did you become a nun?"

"I was twenty-four when I entered the convent. God was calling me so gently I didn't hear Him right away. Why do you ask? You're not contemplating the religious life, are you?"

"No way, Sister. In fifth grade I thought about becoming a nun, but only for about five seconds. I don't want any job where you're not allowed to wear earrings or lip gloss. Nothing personal. It's just that my lips have absolutely no color. I look like walking death if I don't . . ." Once again I caught myself telling her more than I had intended. I shut up and leaned back in my chair.

Sister Clarabelle stood and thanked me again for coming. She flipped her little veil over her shoulder and left the room.

Tracy saw me coming down the hall and ran toward me. She grabbed me by the shoulders and started hurling questions in my face.

"What happened? Did she make you talk about boys and stuff? Did she pump you about if you ever kissed Tim? Did she ask anything about me? Did you confess to having an illegal picture of Bruce Springsteen in your locker? Did you squeal that we really got into Father Damian's room? Did you tell her about me? Am I in any trouble because of this stupid conference? Am I talking too much?"

I just smiled and told her I had promised never to tell anyone what went on in the storeroom, even if they pulled out all my fingernails.

"I hate you, you know that," Tracy said as we walked out to wait for the late bus.

When we got on the bus Tracy pumped me some more. "Can't you tell me anything? Come on, even a little crumb."

"Well, okay. Sister Clarabelle told me she used to work in a department store and wanted to be an artist before she became a nun."

"Yeah, and Sister Marianne wanted to be a rock star before she entered the convent."

The minute I got home I took out my diary and turned to the page where I had written my faults and virtues. I added two virtues to the list and read it over, smiling.

MY VIRTUES

1. Honesty
2. Sense of Humor
3. People can count on me
4. Love my parents
5. ~~Good writer Ha!ha!~~
5. Have Tim for a boyfriend
6. Good head on my shoulders
7. Highly active imagination

I went downstairs and asked Mary if she wanted to play a game of Hungry, Hungry Hippos.

7 Tim was determined to give me another private ski lesson. And I was stalling him since I knew he'd ask me to demonstrate whatever it was he had taught me at the last one.

The whole situation was making me crazy. Like a dream come true, the guy I loved was asking to come over, and I was saying I didn't want to see him. All because of stupid skiing. Who ever invented stupid skiing anyway?

On Wednesday he called and really sounded hurt. "Hey," he said defensively, "if you don't think I'm a good teacher just say so."

I forced a laugh. "Of course you're a good teacher. I just thought your parents might get ticked if you keep asking them to drive you all the way out here."

"Don't worry about it."

"Okay, then come on over and give me a lesson tomorrow night after supper."

"Great!"

I hung up the phone and carried it back to the hall table mumbling to myself.

Joel called to me from the kitchen doorway, "You already hung up the phone. That means you're supposed to stop talking. See, the phone only works when the receiver is lifted off the two little buttons and placed up to the face like this." He made a fist and held it up to his ear.

"Har-dee-har-har. Very funny. But I can't take time to laugh right now, I've got a problem." I told him about how I was going to have to demonstrate what Tim had taught me in last week's lesson, only I had no idea what he had taught me.

"I thought you only function that way in school."

"You're a real gut-buster, Joel. Now come on. Either help me out or be quiet so I can think."

"I'll help you, for a price. You do my paper route for a week if I find out what Tim wants you to show him. Deal?"

"Deal, Dorito breath, but only if I get to keep the tips."

"Okay."

"How're you gonna do it?"

"Don't strain your little brain worrying. Just leave it up to me."

Thursday after school Joel told me that I was supposed to demonstrate a ski move called the wedge. He even demonstrated it for me.

I was about to hug him when he dropped his full newspaper bag around my neck and nearly snapped my neckbone off. The bag weighed a ton.

"Hey," I yelled as he started to head out the door, "you didn't say I had to start today!"

"I didn't say you didn't, either. The list is in the bag. Mrs. Evans just got a Doberman. She told me if I say, 'Sit, Fury,' he'll let me deliver the paper." Joel shut the door behind him.

I rushed through the whole route so I'd have time to memorize the chapter on how to do a wedge before Tim came over. I hoped Mrs. Evans would find her paper at the end of the driveway. Fury didn't seem to understand English.

My lesson with Tim started out great. I had him sit on the den couch while I demonstrated the wedge like crazy. I even threw in a few quotes from the book for good measure.

"How'd I do?" I asked, grinning.

"Fantastic. Boy, either you're some student or I'm some teacher." He got up and came over to me. "Just keep your legs a little farther apart." He pushed outward a little on my knees. "And stand a little straighter," he said as he took my shoulders and pushed them back a little.

He was standing close with his hands on my shoulders. I could feel him looking at my face, but I got so flustered I looked over his shoulder and stared intently at a cobweb drifting down from the corner of the room. He kept looking at me till finally his stare pulled my eyes to his. As he moved his face closer to mine I unbent my knees from the wedge position and stood up straight. He kissed me. Then he abruptly walked over to the couch and started flipping pages in the book real fast, like he was looking for something.

I sat down next to him and closed the book. He looked so sweet, I had to confess about my deal with Joel. Instead of being mad, he grinned.

"You're something, Patty Dillman. You go through the trouble of delivering your brother's papers for a whole week and then confess."

"Wait a minute! I didn't tell you how long I had to deliver papers."

Tim shut his eyes and got a pained expression on his face. "Oh boy, now I did it," he said under his breath. He clasped his hands between his legs and stared intently at the floor.

"I smell two rats," I said. "Two male rats, both of which are in this house right now. Right?"

"Right. And at least one of them is very sorry."

"And the other one is going to be very sorry when I get through with him. Joel found out the information I wanted by telling you the whole story, didn't he? I could have done that my-self!"

"Yeah, he did."

"Okay, look, I'll forgive you for making a horse's rear out of me if you'll promise not to tell Joel I found out. I want to get even in my own way, in my own time."

Tim wasn't too happy about it, but he agreed.

"I think I'd better go," he said. I was so embar-rassed and upset I couldn't even look Tim in the eye. I think he felt the same way. He called his dad to come for him and then we both sat on the den couch, side by side, not saying a word. I got us some Pepsi and we drank it in silence. I could hear every time he swallowed. A couple of times my glass clinked against my teeth and I said, "Excuse me." It took forever for his dad to get there, and when he did, Tim jumped up from the couch and practically raced for the door. This time he didn't take my hands in his or smile or give the thumbs up sign. He just mumbled, " 'Bye" and closed the door behind him.

Joel came downstairs when he heard the door shut. "Hey, partner, how'd it go?" he asked with a big grin on his face.

"Great, partner," I answered, faking a smile. "Thanks for your help. And remember, if you ever need me, I'll be there for you, just like you were there for me."

"Hey, no problem," he said as he disappeared into the kitchen.

I went up to my room and flopped on the bed in the dark, thinking about what squids boys are. After a while there was a knock on my door.

"Yeah?" I asked.

"It's me, Joel."

"I'm sleeping."

He opened the door and came in anyway.

"I said I was sleeping."

"I know but I have to tell you something."

"Yeah?"

"Promise you won't be mad?"

"Of course I don't promise I won't be mad. When you ask me to promise that, it means I probably will be mad."

73

"Promise you won't scratch, hit, kick, or scream at the top of your lungs?"

"No, I do not promise."

"Promise you won't tell Mom or Dad?"

"No!"

"Okay, then I'll tell you. You don't have to do my paper route anymore."

"Oh, that gets me real mad. Please, someone hold me down before I start swinging."

Joel sat down on the floor next to my bed and leaned his head against the wall. I could see the outline of his face in the dim light from the hall. People always say we look a lot alike and when they do, I make a face like I'm going to throw up, but really, we do have the same square jaw and the same mouth with a full lower lip, the same green eyes and even the same nose, kind of rounded at the tip. Joel's hair is curly too and he hates it, just like me. Every morning Mom yells at him for snipping stubborn curls and leaving the hair in the bathroom sink.

Joel put his head down against his chest and said, "The reason you don't have to do my route is that I pulled a rotten trick on you." Then he told me what he had done. He told me he was sorry. He meant it.

I reached out and pushed him over. "How can I be mad at someone as pathetic as you? Get out of here you miserable slug. You're forgiven and for your penance you will type my religion paper if and when I ever get it written. Deal, Dorito breath?"

"Deal, my favorite older sister." He got up and left the room, closing the door quietly behind him.

Some people take all the fun out of getting even.

My first official ski lesson was the next evening at seven o'clock.

As Tracy's dad let us out at the Rec Center his only words of advice were, "Don't let them talk you into thinking you need expensive skis and a designer wardrobe. Parents aren't made of money." Then he winked at me in the rear view mirror.

We waited for the teacher in the gym, standing around a table of coffee, cocoa, and cookies.

I stood in a corner nervously eating a fudge stick, and warned Tracy, "If the teacher looks like he or she was born in any of the Scandinavian countries or brags about learning to ski before learning to walk, I'm leaving."

Of course at that very moment in walked a gorgeous blonde woman, definitely of Norwegian ancestry, who announced that she was the teacher. By way of credentials she told us that she'd been skiing since the age of four. I started to leave but Tracy grabbed my arm and dug her nails into it till I stopped pulling away.

"Now," said Miss Norway, "why don't you introduce yourselves and tell us why you're here."

A middle-aged couple explained that their last child had just left and they were bored; a few young women giggled and said they figured skiing was a good way to meet guys; a few young men said they figured it was a good way to meet girls; Tracy said she was doing it to increase her physical well-being; I said I came because I had a death wish; and the last student, a girl about sixteen, said, and I quote, "I . . . like . . . came because I'm trying to become . . . like . . . whole. I mean . . . like . . . I'm trying to become totally . . . like . . . one with nature. Ya know?"

"Well," said Miss Norway, "I certainly have my work cut out for me, don't I?" We all laughed nervous laughs, the way you do when you want to please the teacher.

I paid more attention to Miss Norway than I had to Tim, because I was paying good money and because she didn't cause shivers to go through me every time she looked at me.

The girl who wanted to get close to nature thought the lesson was "like . . . totally meaningful." The rest of us got through it with a minimum of falling over our own feet. They had these old crummy skis and boots for us to practice with. It took half the lesson to learn how to turn around. We kept stepping on our own skis and each others' and pinning ourselves into weird positions. We also learned the two most basic essentials of skiing—how to fall and how to get up.

When the lesson was over I decided that whoever invented skiing was "like totally mental." I wasn't complaining too much though. At least I got out of the lesson in one piece. As for the next lesson, which would be held on a hill in Easton Valley Park, I wasn't so sure.

When I got home I asked Mom if she was going to St. Luke's the next day.

"Mm-hm," she answered absentmindedly, as she sewed a badge onto Chris's Cub Scout uniform.

"Well, aren't you going to ask me if I want to come?"

She stopped with the needle in midair. "Why on earth would I put myself through your one-hundred-and-one-reasons-why-I-don't-want-to-be-in-the-presence-of-those-bums speech?"

"Well, if you don't want me to come, just say so."

"Of course, I'd love for you to come." Mom put down the uniform and came over to feel my forehead. "No fever," she said. "Did you get a head injury at your ski lesson?"

"Man, this place is full of comedians lately. Is it a crime to want to help people less fortunate than we are? I mean, if it's a crime just say so and we can drop the whole thing."

"I'm sorry, honey. It's very sweet of you to offer. We need all the help we can get, especially now that the weather's getting cold and more people are coming in for a hot meal."

"Well, could you wake me up early tomorrow so I can come?"

"What time?"

"Eight." I didn't tell Mom why, but I wanted to get up early so I would be dressed and have on makeup just in case Tim roller skiied over again.

8 By eleven the next morning, after Mom had sounded the car horn three times, I decided maybe Tim wasn't coming.

I walked slowly, very slowly out to the car.

"What's Mary doing here?" I asked as I slid slowly into the front seat.

"I thought I'd bring her to St. Luke's with us."

"Why, for Pete's sake? What if some of them touch her?"

Mom gave me a dirty look. "A lot of those people are hardly ever around little kids. It does them good to be with Mary. They really enjoy her."

"Well, they'd better not try touching her or anything while I'm around. Hey, what's in all those grocery bags on the floor?"

"Socks. A church donated fifty pairs of socks to St. Luke's. I wish we had more, though. These won't be enough to go around."

I cringed at the thought of handing out the socks. What if the people actually changed their socks right in front of me? And what if they left their old, rotten socks on the floor and Mom made me pick them up? For a minute I considered backing out, but then I remembered Sister Clarabelle and the report I had to write.

"Was Alex there last week?" I asked Mom as we drove.

"Yes, he was, and that reminds me, he asked about you; asked where you were. I told him you hardly ever come."

"Thanks a lot."

"Well, it's the truth."

"Did you ever hear the saying, 'silence is golden'?"

"Yes I have, but I've never known you to subscribe to it." Mom grinned at me and I grinned back.

"Alex was kind of fun, that's all."

When we got to St. Luke's I got the job of stacking the socks on a table at the end of the food line. I dumped the bags out and stood behind the table until my mom came over and whispered that I should move somewhere else because nobody was going to take any of the socks with me standing over them like I was about to give a karate chop to anyone who came near me. So I went into the kitchen and jotted down some notes for my report. I tried to write things Sister Clarabelle would like, so I'd get a good grade:

Saturday. December 10. Today I spent most of the day feeding the hungry and homeless of Easton at St. Luke's Soup Kitchen. I was in charge of distributing warm, clean socks to our city's needy, now that the bitter, cold weather is upon us. Today a few men and women will have cozy feet as well as full stomachs because of the fact that I am doing, not one, but two corporal works of mercy.

I read over what I had written and practically gagged at how phony it was. It didn't seem right to try to get a good grade in religion by being hypocritical.

Just then a wet sponge hit me in the face.

"Very classy way of saying 'hi.' Very classy," I said to Alex as I picked up the sponge and threw it back at him. It hit him in the head and knocked off his baseball hat.

"What a surprise," Alex said, as he jammed the hat back on. "I thought you don't like to come here."

"I don't, but a decent grade in religion class suddenly depends on my coming here a couple more times." I told him about the corporal works of mercy project.

"I don't get it," said Alex. "How can it really be a work of mercy unless it comes from your heart?"

"In the real world, yes. But this is different. This is school. No way do school and the real world have anything to do with each other. Follow me so far?"

"No, but don't let that stop you."

"Look, number one, this whole thing is just a homework assignment. Number two, I didn't choose coming here. Somehow I got cornered into it. And number three, I'm already in deep doo-doo with Sister Clarabelle because of the Never-Never

Land caper. Acing this research project is my only hope of making up points with her. So I'm going to do a good job whether my heart's in it or not. Understand?"

"Let's see. What you're telling me is that this isn't really a work of mercy, it's a research project on the theory of a work of mercy."

"Exactly. Hey, you're pretty quick. How are you at writing term papers?"

"Lousy. But I can help you with the research. I can introduce you to some of the people here. Your report won't be complete without interviews."

I groaned. I was sorry I had told Alex about the report, because now he'd probably tell, and drag me around making me shake hands with every single person in the dining room. He seemed that type.

"No thanks. I wouldn't know what to say to them. I'm bashful," I said.

"And I'm Dopey. Now let's go out and meet Sneezy, Grumpy, Happy, Sleepy, and Doc." He grabbed my arm and started pulling me toward the dining hall.

"I'll start off with an easy one. You'll like my good buddy, Charles. He's my favorite person here."

When we walked into the dining room every single person there looked up. Alex deposited me in a folding chair right next to one of the men. Then he went to the other side of the long table and sat opposite me.

"Charles, I'd like you to meet my friend, Bashful," Alex said to the man I had been dumped next to.

"Pleased to meet you, young lady. Call me Charles, if you'd like. Can't tolerate Charlie or Chuck. Don't hanker to nicknames much. What do they call you besides Bashful? You got a certified name?"

I was so embarrassed I wanted to crawl under the table. And while I was under there I wanted to bite Alex's leg. But I said, "Yes I do have a certified, I mean a real name. It's Patricia. And I'm pleased to meet you."

"Well, I must confess, Bashful fits you a mite better. Look up, girl, let's see your pretty eyes."

I lifted my head and looked at Charles. He had the most piercing blue eyes I have ever seen, pale, pale blue, framed by a red, rough face with a few days' growth of dark stubbly beard. His lips were chapped and his thick, brown hair was matted and dirty. He had a small scar above one eyebrow. He wore an overcoat that had stains all over it. One pocket was ripped half off and the coat had no buttons. It was held closed by a length of rope. When he reached out to shake my hand, his was coarse and cold and very dry. I tried to figure out how old he was but I couldn't. Charles could have been thirty or fifty for all I could tell.

Charles introduced me to his friend Stubs, who was small and dark and smiled a lot. He had dark, greasy hair and wore a brown wool hat with ear flaps.

"I ain't got no certified name," Stubs told me, between short, nervous puffs on a cigarette. "Or maybe I do, but it ain't in my recollections."

"Stubs is just about as dumb a human being as you'll ever meet. Right Stubs?" Charles announced to me, and Stubs smiled and nodded his head like he had been paid the highest compliment of his life.

"I'd a been dead fifty times over by now, weren't for Charles taking care of me," Stubs said with a grin.

Charles went back to eating his dinner and Stubs proceeded to do exactly what I had been afraid of. He started to change his socks fumblingly right at the table.

"Here, let me help you," Alex offered. I scowled at them both, then got up and went into the kitchen.

Later, Alex came back and asked me why I had left so abruptly. He actually thought I should have sat there in plain view of Stubs's naked feet and interviewed him.

"Yeah," I said in an annoyed voice. "And what was I supposed to ask? Was I supposed to ask Stubs why the tips of three of his fingers are missing?"

"You could have. And he would have told you the story of how a friend of his once held an ax over Stubs' hand and bet him that he couldn't pull his hand out of the way before the ax hit it. Stubs almost won the bet. If he hadn't been drunk he probably would have. Stubs belongs in a psychiatric hospital, but he got discharged even though he wasn't completely well."

"And what about that old couple holding hands all the time? Was I supposed to ask them if they just got off the Love Boat?"

"Just because they're old and poor doesn't mean they aren't capable of love, Patty."

"And Charles? Should I have walked up to him and politely inquired how he got to be a bum?"

"You know darned well you could have asked him a hundred other questions. But if you're so curious, I'll tell you how he got into the situation he's in. He was at a family picnic with his wife and daughter a long time ago. He had a few beers so he asked his wife to drive on the way home. They ended up in a car accident and his wife and daughter died. Charles blames himself and he doesn't care about anything anymore."

"Oh," was all I could say.

"Look, Patty, I know you're just here for your religion project, but as long as you're here, open your eyes. You're one of the privileged few of the world and your life was handed to you. So don't be too smug and don't look down your nose at anyone."

Alex picked up a stack of dirty plates and carried it to a big garbage can. As he scraped leftovers from the plates he kept on lecturing me. "We know these people have all kinds of problems and are here for all kinds of reasons. But we volunteer here because we don't think anyone should be hungry. Period. No judgments. And if you can't accept that, you may as well go do your project someplace else."

My face felt hot and my eyes burned. I walked away from Alex to the huge stainless steel sink. I turned on the hot water faucet, squeezed out some detergent and started to attack a mountain of dirty dishes. Tears of anger and humiliation plopped into the suds. Alex had no right talking to me like that. He was telling me not to judge people, but he was judging me. It was none of his business what I thought or how I felt. I decided I would never speak to him again until he apologized.

When I finished the dishes, I peeked into the dining room to see if Mary was all right. Alex was there playing chess with Charles. Mary was sitting on a chair next to Charles, watching him as he studied the board. Stubs was sitting with them smiling. A few other guys were gathered around watching, pretending they knew what was going on in the game.

9 I spent almost the whole hour at church on Sunday trying to think of a topic for my monthly column in the school newspaper. All during seventh grade I had bugged the newspaper advisor, Mr. Lampert, to let me do a column. He finally got sick of my whining and agreed to let me write one on a trial basis this year.

My first column had poked fun at the seventh graders and had gotten me into major trouble with the whole seventh-grade class. My second column had been about friendship and had helped to patch up a problem between Tracy and me. Now it was December and my third column was due in Mr. Lampert's mailbox the next day. Which is why I was trying to think of an idea instead of praying during church.

My only major interruption was Mary falling off the kneeler and biting her tongue open. Of course she chose to fall while my mother and father were up at the altar helping to give out Communion.

"Don't you dare scream," I whispered as I fished her out from halfway under the pew. She answered with a gut-busting wail right into my ear. Now I knew how Tim had felt when I screamed on the phone.

Then Mary proceeded to bleed all over my pink fleece jacket. I couldn't believe the amount of blood that can come from a little kid's tongue. I fumbled around in my pockets for a tissue to press against the blood on my jacket. Then I found a second crumpled up piece and pushed it against her mouth. We marched down the middle aisle with everyone's eyes on us.

The instant we got out of sight of the congregation she shut up, as if on cue, smiled at me, and ate the tissue.

"Why me?" I sighed and dug through my purse for another one.

On the way home from church my father stopped at a pet store and bought Mary two little fish, a fish bowl, fish food, a plastic plant, and a deep sea diver decoration to put in the bowl, all because she bit her tongue. While we were in the store I asked for a cocker spaniel, but would Dad buy it for me? No. I even showed him an ugly paper cut I had gotten at school, but he didn't care about my injuries.

When we got home I ran up to my room and sat down at my desk to think up a column idea. Of course nothing came to me. So I called my genius friend Jeannie to help me out.

"Boy, am I glad you asked," she said, sounding angry. "Write about book slobs. I'm sitting here reading a book I took out of St. Iggie's library and on practically every page there's some sort of stain or blob or clump of decomposed food. It's disgusting. I took four books out last week and every one

88

of them is the same. Write about how the librarians should inspect the books being returned and charge a slob fine."

Jeannie would have gone on, but I cut in and told her to calm down. "I'll try to break this to you gently, Jeannie. You're probably the only one in the entire school including the librarian who'd read a column on slob fines. It isn't exactly a hot topic."

Next I called Tracy to see if she had any bright ideas.

"I keep trying to empty out my mind so an idea will come floating in, but all that floats in is how I love Tim and hate skiing," I complained.

"Well, there's your idea. Write about how you hate skiing. In fact, write about how you hate sports. Write about how you're a sports wimp. Write about how you're turning into a total couch potato. Write . . ."

"All right, already. I get the idea. Why don't you quit before you start insulting me."

After we hung up I went upstairs and wrote on a fresh sheet of filler paper:

Bits and Pieces
By Patricia Dillman

Before I could write any more, Chris came barging in wanting to stump me with some stupid brainteaser.

"I bet you fifty cents you won't be able to get this one," he said with a grin on his face.

"Bet's on," I agreed. Chris's brainteasers are always so old I've heard them a million times before.

"Okay. Here it is. An electric train is traveling west at thirty miles an hour. The wind is blowing south at thirty miles an hour. Which way is the smoke from the train blowing?"

"It isn't. An electric train doesn't have any smoke."

"Bet's off," he said quickly and ran out of the room.

"Hey, no fair you creep," I yelled after him.

I went back to thinking about how to start my column. Ten seconds later Chris came storming in again.

"Okay I've got a harder one. I bet you a dollar you won't get this one."

"Bet's on."

"A plane is flying east from California to New York. It crashes exactly on the border of Utah and Colorado. In which state do they bury the survivors?"

"Neither state. You don't bury survivors. Pay up, loser."

"Bet's off," he shouted as he ran out of my room.

"You weasel! That's the last time I make a bet with you! And keep out of my room. I'm trying to think!"

A few minutes later he stuck his head in the doorway again.

"Okay I've got the best one yet. I bet you two dollars you won't get this one."

"No thank you, Mr. Cheater."

"I won't go back on the bet this time."

"Promise?"

"Promise."

"Scout's honor?"

"Scout's honor." He held up three fingers as he said it.

"Okay, bet's on. What's your latest dumb brain-teaser?"

"A policeman was walking by a woman's apartment. He heard the woman scream, 'John, don't shoot me.' Then he heard a gunshot. He ran into the apartment. The woman was lying on the floor dead. In the room with her were four people: a milkman, an airplane pilot, a doctor, and an army officer. The policeman immediately arrested the milkman. Why?"

I had never heard this one before.

"The policeman knew the milkman's name was John," I guessed.

"No. Two more guesses."

"The policeman knew the woman was having an affair with her milkman."

"What's an affair?"

"Never mind."

"Whatever it is, it's wrong anyway. One more guess."

"There were milk fingerprints on the gun."

"Wrong. I win two dollars! The policeman arrested the milkman because the airplane pilot, the doctor, and the army officer were all women, dummy."

"Bet's off!" I hollered as he ran down the hall laughing hysterically.

I had a hard time getting my concentration back. I sat there staring at my paper and biting my nails while I tried to think. Finally, after two hours, my column was finished. It came out like this:

Bits and Pieces
By Patricia Dillman

I've just been called a sports wimp. And it's true, I have absolutely no interest in any sport more difficult than thumb wrestling. But maybe there's nothing wrong with me. Maybe it's the rest of the world that's gone crazy.

Part of the nightly news on TV every day is about sports. One whole page of our school newspaper is dedicated to sports. A whole section of the daily newspaper is taken up by sports. What's the big deal? Why don't they use some of that precious space for important news like updates on all the soap operas?

Take football, for example. All the players do is gang up on the guy with the ball and try to smash him into the ground by jumping on his head, stomach, and other important body parts. Aren't there laws against that kind of thing?

And those helmets. I can't imagine anyone's hair looking good after they take one of those things off, even if they used a whole can of hairspray before the game. I'm here to tell you that even the spectators aren't safe. I once got hit in the face with a football while sitting in the stands, and was knocked unconscious. Take my word for it, football is not a fun pastime.

Wrestling is just as barbaric. Each player grabs the other one anywhere he pleases and tries to whap him down onto the floor and then crawl on top of him with his sweaty body. Please, I don't want to talk about it anymore. I just ate.

Basketball is dumb, not to mention impolite. I don't like a sport where they trip each other and then pretend they didn't mean it, and wave their hands in front of the other guy's face right when he's trying to aim for a basket. Playing this game has got to be discouraging. Your team can score over a hundred points and still lose. No thank you.

Soccer is the other extreme. You can win with a score of one point. However, to succeed in soccer it has to be your life's wish to become brain damaged. I mean, the players all have perfectly capable hands. Why don't they use them, for heaven's sake? Why do they have to scramble their brains by hitting the ball with their heads?

Baseball isn't as vicious as some of the other sports. Nobody hits you or pushes you down. You just mind your own business. But did you ever notice that no one in the stands really cares what happens? They just come to eat.

Then there's skiing, a sport that should only be attempted wearing a full suit of armor. I mean, we're talking about sailing down a hill at one hundred miles an hour on two giant Popsicle sticks with no brakes on them. We're also talking about snow blowing down your neck, wind chapping your face, and cold turning your fingers and toes blue. We're talking about possible crutches, casts, and concussions.

So what's left? Tennis. The outfits are cute, the scoring is cute, but I have a sneaking feeling you could break a fingernail if you got carried away trying to hit the ball.

Like I said, it's the rest of you who are crazy, not me. Now you'll have to excuse me while I go do some thumb exercises. The tournament is tomorrow.

I read what I had written and decided it was a gem. I put it in my backpack and picked up *Romeo and Juliet*. I had vowed not to get behind in my reading. But I couldn't concentrate. My mind kept pulling back to the column. Finally I got it out of my backpack and read it again. I took a pencil and crossed out the section on skiing.

I picked up *Romeo and Juliet.* After a few minutes I pulled the column out of my backpack again and erased all the lines I had drawn through the skiing part of my column. Hey, it was all in fun and if Tim didn't have a sense of humor that was his problem. Back to *Romeo and Juliet.* Five minutes later, back to the column to cross out the skiing section again. By the time I finished, the paper was a mess, but the section on skiing was crossed out in the final copy.

I knew I was being a wimp. But I didn't want to risk Tim's reaction.

I gave up on *Romeo and Juliet* and spent the rest of the day trying to send brain waves to Tim to make him want to call me. It didn't work. Even when I sat on the floor next to the phone with my eyes shut tight, pressing my temples and willing Tim to get my extrasensory message, the only result I got was Mary plopping her little body in front of me and playing "Peek-a-boo."

10 As we stood waiting for the bus on Monday morning, stamping our feet every few seconds to keep them warm, I said to Tracy, "This ski plan better work. Tim hasn't called me since Thursday night's private ski lesson."

"Why don't you call him?" she asked.

"Because he's the one who owes an apology."

Tracy shrugged her shoulders like she didn't think it was important who made the call.

"He hates me. I know it," I went on. "He thinks I'm a loser. He saw me looking gross in my father's robe. Then he got upset with me when I found out his plot with Joel. Not to mention the fact that I'm not interested in anything he likes. Plus I'm borderline ugly. He definitely hates me. Tracy, this ski thing better work. I'd die if I lost him!"

I felt a sudden rush of panic. I wondered what the girls at the lunch table would think if Tim broke up with me. They'd probably think I was a real loser. And pretty soon the whole school would hear about it and everyone would think I was a real loser, except maybe for Gary Holmes. I'd be forced to drop out of St. Iggie's.

Tracy put her arm around my shoulder. "Get hold of yourself. It's all going to work out. I told Scott about the ski trip to Benton over Christmas vacation, and he and Tim are planning to go. When we go on that ski trip you two are going to be like this." She crossed two of her fingers. "Trust me. Have I ever steered you wrong before?"

I groaned.

We got on the bus and found an empty seat. Gary Holmes came down the aisle, squished himself into our seat, leaned over Tracy and said, "Hey, dollface, what's this about a ski trip?"

"None of your business, chopped-liver face," Tracy answered for me.

Gary ignored her and spoke to me again. "If someone's planning a ski trip, count me in."

"This is a private ski trip, for humans only, so forget it," Tracy answered.

Gary gave her a dirty look, then stared into my face with his eyebrows raised till I told him about the trip.

"I don't think we have anything to worry about," Tracy whispered, "Gary'll probably spend the whole time trying to figure out which ski goes on which foot. He won't have time to butt into your love life. Hey, I meant to ask you, want to go to the mall today and get a few more holes pierced in our ears?"

"What?" I shrieked, so loud the bus driver slammed on the brakes and Gary fell off the corner of our seat into the aisle.

"Sorry, Mr. Bonenfant," I called. "I was . . . I was . . . eating gummy bears and I almost choked on one. I'm okay now. Everything's fine. You can drive on." I smiled weakly.

Mr. Bonenfant didn't drive on. He glared at me

for, I bet, sixty seconds before he said, "You want to walk the rest of the way to school? You can choke at the top of your lungs the whole five miles."

"No, really, I'm okay now." I coughed lightly. "See, all clear." I smiled again. I wanted to die. Mr. Bonenfant slowly turned around and stepped on the gas. The bus was as quiet as a church. I looked straight ahead and said out of the corner of my mouth, "Do you realize that 99 percent of the grief in my life is caused by you, Tracy Gilmore?"

Tracy was trying hard not to laugh. "Boy, some friend you are," she said, "eating gummy bears and not offering me any."

"Stuff it, Trace. Now what is this about getting more holes pierced in our ears? If we trotted into school with earrings dangling off every square inch of our earlobes we'd get booted out so fast we wouldn't know what hit us!"

"Why?" Tracy asked calmly. "There's nothing in the rule book that tells the number of holes we're allowed to have in our ears."

"There's also nothing in the rule book that says shaved heads are against the rules, or purple hair, or tattoos, or girls sneaking over to the priests' floor. Certain things are left up to common sense, which obviously we didn't get any of when they passed it out. But I'm trying."

"Well, do you want to do it or don't you? Do you

or don't you want to look so awesome that Tim will fall at your feet and worship you?"

"I do not. And I call the twenty-four-hour rule on this conversation."

"Boy, sometimes you act like a total wimp," Tracy complained.

"That's how wimps are supposed to act."

At that point Gary butted in again to tell me that, speaking of Tim, he had seen him at Benton on Sunday, going up the lift with a gorgeous blonde.

"Look, low-life," Tracy sputtered at him, "I know you can't find any of your own kind to sit with, because there aren't any of your own kind on this planet, but would you mind moving to some other seat?" She gave him a jab that knocked him onto the floor with a thud. He got up and headed farther down the aisle.

"Don't pay any attention to him, Pats. He's just jealous of you and Tim."

We were quiet the rest of the ride to school. When the bus stopped at St. Iggie's, Tracy turned to me and asked innocently, "Did I hear you say there's no rule against tattoos? Wouldn't a little butterfly right about here be dynamite?" She touched her cheek.

I stared at her for a minute, not knowing if she was kidding or serious, till she burst out laughing.

"Tracy," I said, "you are a cruel, mentally deranged, underhanded rat."

"Thank you," she said sweetly as she got up and headed to the door.

That night my dad took me to pick up my rental ski equipment. As soon as I got home I took the skis to the basement to try them on. Chris came down to watch so I showed him how to turn on them and how to move around without getting tangled up. I pretended I was the different people in my class and showed Chris how we all made fools of ourselves at the first lesson.

After a while Mom yelled down that Chris should have been in bed an hour ago.

"Tim didn't call while I was out, did he?" I asked as Chris scooted up the stairs.

"Yeah he did," I heard Chris say from the kitchen.

"What?" I started to run after him and fell flat on my face trying to go upstairs wearing skis. I unclipped the boots and took off after him. I tackled him just as he reached the doorway to his room.

"Are you pulling my leg?" I asked through gritted teeth. " 'Cause if you are, I'll break off both of your legs and hit you over the head with them. Now tell the truth, did Tim call?"

"Yeah," Chris answered, almost in a whisper.

"Why didn't you tell me?"

"I forgot."

"What did he say?"

"Nothing."

"Nothing? He just called and breathed into the phone and didn't say a single word? Chris, you better remember."

"Well, he . . . he said, 'Hi, Chris' and . . . 'Is Patty there?' and . . . and . . . 'So long, Buddy.' " Chris smiled as if he was very pleased with himself.

"Did he say he'd call back?"

"I can't remember." Chris started to bawl so I loosened my stranglehold on his knees and put my arm around him.

"Okay, don't get upset. Just think calmly. Try to remember."

"I can't."

"Did you write anything down on the message pad by the phone, where you're supposed to write down who called and who the call was for and if there was a message, and Dad always warns you that if you don't, you won't be allowed to answer the phone anymore? Did you do that?"

"I forgot."

I looked at my watch. It was 9:45. I made a dash for the phone. Of course Joel was using it.

"Could you hurry it up? I've got to make an important call." Joel waved me away and dialed furiously. A few seconds later he started dialing again. Then again.

"Could you practice dialing some other time? I need to use the phone. It's a matter of life and death. Chris's."

Joel ignored me and kept up his non-stop dialing.

"What the heck are you doing, calling outer Mongolia or something?" I tried to grab the phone out of his hand.

"Flake off, flake," he said, still holding the phone to his ear. "I'm dialing station WTNT. The tenth caller wins two pizzas from Pizza Shack." He kept dialing.

"Look, I hate to be the one to break this to you, but the tenth caller has probably picked up his pizzas and eaten them by now. Give it up." Joel dialed three more times before he handed me the phone. I dialed Tim's number. His mother answered and said Tim was in bed.

I wondered if Chris realized that his days on this planet were numbered.

11 The cost of renting skis for the season had wiped out most of my bank account, and I was starting to get nervous wondering how I was going to cough up the money for the ski trip. Mom and Dad had offered to pay $50 as part of my Christmas present, but I was going to have to put in $100 plus spending money. My bank book read $37.63.

We were at lunch on Tuesday when I said to Tracy, "I'm almost afraid to ask, but do you have any bright ideas about where we're going to get the money for the trip? It's less than two weeks away, you know."

Tracy smiled. "Of course. I'm getting a paper route. And if I start right away I'll get to hand out those calendars that say 'Season's Greetings From Your Newspaper Carrier' on the front. If you use strategy you can make big bucks off those calendars. You hand them out right before Christmas when people are in a generous mood and you pick a real snowy day so people will feel sorry for you. If it's cold enough, after a few minutes you get a runny nose and that helps even more. Lucinda Wasco told me she hauled in a total of $135 last year."

"You're forgetting one minor detail," I said. "You've got a snowball's chance in hell of getting a route at this time of year. No kid would be stupid enough to give up a route at calendar time."

"Oh, I'll get a route, don't worry about that," Tracy said, still smiling. With Tracy's luck, she probably would. But I had no intention of even trying. No way was I going to drag a bunch of papers from door to door every single day and get my hands all smudged with black ink and run the risk of having anyone I know see me.

I know from Joel's route what a rough job it is. One day a dog took a chomp out of my bag and the owners blamed me for scaring their dog. And whenever I do Joel's route I always end up with some spare papers, which means I forgot some houses. Then, right in the middle of supper the customers start calling to complain, and my mother makes my father drive the papers to the houses and he gets mad at me and says things like, "I hope you remember this the next time I ask you to shovel the driveway, young lady."

So I had to figure out some other way of making seventy dollars. After school I tried casually asking my mother to loan me the money. It didn't work.

"Why don't you get a babysitting job?" she suggested.

I thought about it and decided it wasn't a bad idea to have someone pay me for watching their television set and eating their food. Plus I could talk on their phone for hours without Joel yanking at the cord under the closet door every two seconds.

I put on my jacket and ran over to the college student union where there's a wall-sized bulletin board full of notices and ads. Most of them were from college kids wanting to share a ride home for the Christmas break. But I did find two babysitting jobs being offered:

Wanted: Babysitter for three active pre-schoolers. Mon., Wed., Fri. 3–6 p.m.
Call Mrs. Ward at 555–1221

and

Lindsay Marie, aged four, is looking for a caring, loving babysitter who likes to play Candyland, read stories, and have tea parties. Her mom usually does these things with her but has to attend class on Tuesdays and Thursdays from 3–6 p.m. If you're interested, call Lindsay or her mom at 555–3567.

I decided to call Mrs. Ward, mainly because Lindsay Marie's ad made me want to throw up.

Mrs. Ward sounded very nice and friendly. She told me that she and her husband taught at the college and she needed a babysitter for the times when their schedules overlapped.

"The kids can be a handful," she said. "There's Max, who's four. He's quiet and shy, but don't let that fool you. Take your eyes off him for a minute and he'll tie you to your chair and head for the bus station. The twins, Elaine and Eileen, are one year old. They sleep most of the afternoon. But when they're up you wish you had four legs and eight arms. Do you have any experience babysitting?"

I told her about Chris and Mary and said I'd love the job.

"Wonderful. Can you start ASAP?"

"Sure," I said.

"Then I'll expect you tomorrow at three. The address is 30 Alumni Drive."

I hung up the phone and ran to find my mother so I could ask what ASAP means. It means "as soon as possible" and luckily I could start ASAP because detention had ended the Friday before.

All day Wednesday I felt a little nervous. I was about to begin my first real job, and I hoped I wouldn't blow it. But the day seemed doomed even before I got to the Wards' house.

The bad luck started during last period. We were sitting there waiting for the end-of-period bell to ring, when the teacher got called out of the room for a few minutes. The minute she left, Heidi Weber, who was voted class clown last year, decided to be funny. She threw a pencil up as hard as she could, so the point stuck in the soft, acoustic tile ceiling. Of course, every other moron in the room had to go and do the same thing. Pretty soon pencils were hanging down from the ceiling like icicles.

I was not going to take part in such a childish scheme. Besides, the only thing I had on me was my silver Cross pen with Patricia Dillman inscribed on it that my grandmother gave me when I graduated from elementary school.

Before I could stop her, spaghetti-brain Joyce Nesmith grabbed my pen and shot it at the ceiling. It stuck up there like a signed confession that I had taken part in the fun.

I jumped up, called Joyce a spaghetti brain and climbed on my desk to try and reach the pen. I stretched till I thought my arm would pull out of its socket, but the pen was out of my reach. Just then the "spotter" yelled, "She's coming!" So we all had to sit down and act like angels.

We held our breath hoping none of the icicles would fall. The bell rang and we all stood up and walked out of room 212 very slowly, trying not to make a breeze. The minute we hit the hall we beat it fast.

I didn't have time to try to retrieve my icicle after school. I had to catch the early bus. So I left with the uncomfortable feeling that Sister Clarabelle would be waiting for me at the door the next morning with a frown on her face and a message to go to the principal's office, where I would be presented with my pen and a membership renewal in the detention club.

I had no desire to experience detention again, even though the regulars were kind of fascinating, and some of them turned out to be okay kids. On the late bus every day, a couple of them taught Tracy and me how to play poker and showed us some very creative ways to cheat on tests. I swear, it takes more time and thought to come up with cheating methods than it takes to study. I didn't have the nerve to share that bit of wisdom with them, though.

At exactly three o'clock I rang the Wards' doorbell. Mrs. Ward invited me in and introduced me to Max. Max, who looked like a miniature football player, ran behind the couch. Mrs. Ward and I tiptoed upstairs where she showed me the twins, sleeping side by side in one crib. One of them was sucking gently on the other one's thumb. They looked adorable.

When Mrs. Ward left, the twins were still sleeping peacefully and Max was still behind the couch. I decided the job was going to be a piece of cake.

"And speaking of cake," I said out loud, "let's check out the food supply."

The refrigerator was loaded with great stuff. I filled a bowl with peanut butter cup ice cream and spritzed a mountain of Reddi-Wip on top. We *never* have Reddi-Wip at home, not since the time Mom caught Joel and me spraying it directly into our mouths.

Then I cut myself a humungous slice of chocolate-frosted chocolate cake and poured a tall glass of Tab. I don't care much for diet drinks, but beggars can't be choosers.

I set up a TV table in front of the couch, flicked on the TV set and made myself comfortable.

I had just stuffed a forkful of cake into my mouth when I heard a car pull into the driveway. I looked out the window and there was Mrs. Ward coming toward the house. In a panic, I grabbed a *Newsweek* magazine from the coffee table, opened it up and dumped my cake into it. I slapped the magazine shut, sat on it to flatten it out, and put it at the bottom of a pile of magazines on the coffee table. I poured the Tab into a potted plant, slid the bowl of ice cream under the couch, flicked off the set and was just folding the table up when Mrs. Ward walked in the side door.

"Forgot my notes," she said, and disappeared upstairs. After she had left for the second time I stood at the living room window shaking like a leaf and watching for about fifteen minutes to make sure she didn't come back again. When I finally reached under the couch for my ice cream, it had disappeared. I knelt on the couch and peered over the back. There was Max, smiling, his whole face covered with peanut butter cup ice cream.

"Oh well, kid. At least I didn't get caught making a complete oink-oink out of myself. Let's go clean you up." I hauled him up and carried him to the kitchen, where it suddenly hit me that, unless

Mrs. Ward was totally blind, I had been caught after all. Mrs. Ward had come through the kitchen where all the evidence of my food binge lay spread out on the counter: ice cream carton, Reddi-Wip can, cake, empty bottle of Tab. I wanted to die.

I took the *Newsweek* magazine out to the garage and buried it at the bottom of a trash can, feeling like a total jerk. I mean, Mrs. Ward did tell me to help myself to anything I wanted. But now she couldn't miss the fact that I'd vaporized her entire week's food supply in five minutes.

I sighed as I turned the doorknob to go back into the kitchen. The door wouldn't open. After a few minutes of banging and pounding I accepted the fact that locking me out was Max's idea of a joke. I raced through the garage and around to the front door. It was locked. I ran to the sliding door at the back of the house. It was locked, too. Inside I could see Max sitting on the living room floor with his face inside the ice cream carton, licking it clean.

I tapped on the glass. No answer. I banged on the glass. No answer. I yelled through the glass, but Max just looked at me, grinned, and stuck his head back into the ice cream carton.

It doesn't take much to put me in a panic, and pretty soon I was in a full-blown state of terror. What if the twins were awake and screaming their heads off? What if one of them stopped breathing? What if Max decided to set fire to the house after he finished his ice cream? What if Mr. or Mrs. Ward called home and Max told them I'd left?

I started to cry. Max waved at me. That's when I got my idea. I swiped at the tears running down my cheeks and waved back at him, trying to fake a smile.

"Max," I yelled. "I just got a great idea. I'm going to borrow your sled and go over to Liberty Hill. Is that okay?" Liberty Hill is the place on campus where the students go sledding on cafeteria trays, even though it's forbidden.

Max came over and pressed his nose against the sliding door. I picked up a red plastic sled that was leaning against the back of the house and dusted the snow off it. I started to walk away, then stopped and came back.

"Want to come?" I asked, as if the thought had just struck me. Max clicked the lock. I pulled the door open and lunged inside. Then I started to cry again and shake all over. Meanwhile Max was busily trying to put on his snow pants. I told him we'd better wait till the twins got up.

Luckily, he didn't throw a tantrum or anything. He took the snow pants off and announced, "Fingerpaint."

"No fingerpaints. Not right now. Let's do a puzzle, instead."

"Fingerpaints."

"Puzzle."

"Fingerpaints."

"How about Legos?"

"Fingerpaints."

"Legos, and that's final. I should tie you to a chair after what you pulled, Maxo, so just knock it off with the fingerpaints and let's build a castle out of Legos." I dragged out a huge can of Legos from behind the couch and started snapping them together, till Max came over and joined in.

As soon as he was busy building, I collapsed on the couch and called Tracy to advise her never to consider babysitting as a career. I told her everything that had happened in the last hour and pretty soon we were both laughing hysterically.

As usual we got to talking about Tim and Scott. Then we got into how Karen Brandt is making a fool of herself over Karl Dubiel and Karl couldn't care less about her. We were discussing Suzanne Nugent's new haircut when I had to hang up because I heard the twins howling.

I changed their diapers, put them in the playpen in the living room and looked around for Max. I found him in the kitchen, happily fingerpainting all over the kitchen table with pancake syrup. Right then I decided two things: I was never going to have children, and I was never coming back to babysit for the Wards.

Just as I got the syrup mess cleaned up I heard a muffled cry from the vicinity of the living room. Elaine (or Eileen) was sitting on her sister's face, suffocating her. Then Max started putting on his snow pants again. This time he did throw a tantrum when I told him I was too tired to take him sledding.

Of course Mrs. Ward walked in right then. But you know something? She smiled.

"I'll bet you decided this afternoon that you're never going to have kids, right?"

I didn't answer.

"Just tell me everything went fine and the kids were good and you had no problems. Lie to me," she said. She gave my shoulder a squeeze and pressed a ten-dollar bill into my hand. I did some quick calculating and figured I could earn fifty dollars by Christmas. That plus my allowance would make up the money I needed.

I laughed and told her everything went fine and the kids were good and I had no problems. I told her I'd be back for round two on Friday.

I went home and gave Mary a big hug.

12 Friday evening, after a hard day of school and babysitting, I sat on the living-room couch biting my nails while I waited for Mom to drive me to my first outdoor ski lesson. While I waited I tried to figure out how I had gotten myself talked into ski lessons.

Next to me, Mary was busily trying to force a Barbie evening gown onto a Ken doll. I knew she'd start whining any second and then work herself up to a wail and finally into her world-famous gut-busting scream. I didn't need any more stress at that moment so I tried to explain the problem.

"Honey," I said patiently, "Ken is the boy. Barbie is the girl. Even if you managed to wedge that gown on Ken, which is highly unlikely, I don't think Barbie would want to be seen with him. Boys who dress like girls get called funny names."

"What names?" she wanted to know.

"Never mind what names. Just take my word for it. The red satin strapless gown belongs on Barbie. The black pants and jacket belong on Ken."

She ignored me and kept trying to jam Ken's hips into the gown. Of course the thing ripped right down the seam and she proceeded to scream her head off.

"Told you," I said and went back to biting my nails. Chris walked in, looked at me and walked back out again yelling, "Mom, Patty's biting her nails!" Mom ignored his tattling, as usual. A few minutes later I heard him yell from the kitchen, "Mom, Joel's drinking milk right out of the container." Mom ignored him, as usual.

Finally, when I was about to jump out of my skin from nerves, Mom said she was ready to leave.

There were four classes of students at Easton Valley Park, spread out at the bottom of a hill that looked like Mount Everest from where I stood, although Miss Norway called it a beginner slope.

We stood at the bottom while she taught us the ill-fated wedge that I had demonstrated for Tim. She also showed us how to stop and told us how to hold onto the tow rope that we would be using to get up tonight's hill.

"Okay, is everybody ready?" she asked enthusiastically. No one answered except Tracy, who waved her ski poles in the air and answered an excited, "Yeahhhh!"

"You're a sick person," I whispered.

Tracy volunteered to be the first on the tow rope, a long pulley-like rope that you cling to for dear life while it slowly moves you up the hill.

I got so panicked about the possibility of being separated from Tracy that I grabbed on to the rope right behind her.

"Remember," called Miss Norway, "keep your

skis pointed straight. Keep your poles tucked under your arm. Hold on tight. And everybody wait for me at the top." Where did she think we were planning on going?

The rope slowly dragged our line of human sacrifices up the hill. Tracy was first, I was second and about half a dozen people were behind me. All of a sudden the rope jerked. I got so scared I let go. I sat down hard and started to fall over backward down the hill, taking everyone but Tracy with me. Head over skis, we all went tumbling back to Miss Norway.

She checked hysterically to make sure no one had gotten hurt, then let everyone but me go back on the rope. She taught me how to side-step and made me go up the whole slope that way. It was humiliating.

When we were all assembled at the top she showed us how to turn our skis so we were all facing the same direction—down.

"Now," she said, "you'll go down one at a time, doing the wedge. Remember, pigeon-toed stance. Tips together. Tails of skis apart. Flexed knees. The more you spread your feet apart, the slower you'll go. Everybody got that?"

Again, Tracy yelled, "Yeahh!" The rest of us just stood there looking petrified.

"Good," said Miss Norway, as if we had all answered. "When I call on you to go down, just give a little push with your poles to get you started moving. Does anyone want to be first?"

I turned to signal Tracy that she shouldn't dare offer to go first and leave me. As I turned and lifted my pole toward her, a horrible, terrible, unbelievably frightening thing happened. I felt my body start to move forward, down the hill. I couldn't stop. I couldn't scream. I was paralyzed with fear. All I could hear was Tracy cheering, "Yeahhh, Patty! Way to go, hot dog!"

Faster and faster my skis carried me down the hill.

"Wedge! Wedge!" Miss Norway called through cupped hands. I tried desperately to command my body to wedge, to command my brain to remember how, to picture myself demonstrating the wedge to Tim in my den. But all that came into my head was Tim holding my shoulders and kissing me.

A scream finally came out of my mouth. "Help! I'm gonna die!" The wind carried my words away. I was alone, flying down the hill, picking up speed moment by moment.

"Helpppp!" I yelled again, in one long, desperate cry till there was no breath left in me. I wanted to close my eyes, but I couldn't. They were fixed on an enormous fir tree at the bottom of the hill that was going to slow me down to an abrupt and final stop.

I knew I was going to die. And I'll tell you, your life does not flash before your eyes like they tell you. Either that or I hadn't done anything in my lifetime interesting enough to flash into my mind.

Suddenly I felt something grabbing me under

each armpit. I started to slow down. "Easy does it. Easy does it," I heard Miss Norway say.

"You're all right," another voice said soothingly. I looked to my right. I looked to my left. Miss Norway and some guy who had an instructor's jacket on were holding my arms and, miraculously, I slowed down to a stop a few feet in front of the fir tree.

"She's okay!" Miss Norway hollered up to my classmates. Then she turned to me and told me to sit down. She took off my skis.

"Put your head down between your legs," she ordered. "You're going to be fine. You're just shaken up that's all. When you feel better, you'd better go wait inside the shelter."

"No. I want to go back up the hill. I'll never ski again if I don't." The thought that I could have gotten myself killed or worse didn't matter. All that mattered was that I had to learn to ski to keep from losing Tim.

Still shaking, I side-stepped back up the hill to the sound of cheers and cries of "hot dog," and "atta girl."

When everyone else had wedged down, Miss Norway took my arms and positioned me for my second run. She skiied backward down the hill, right in front of me, all the way.

It was humiliating.

13 When I woke up Saturday morning every muscle in my body ached from the ski lesson. I didn't want to go to the soup kitchen. I didn't even want to get out of bed for the next ten years.

But I managed to drag myself up, get dressed and put on makeup, just in case Tim stopped by like he had done two Saturdays ago.

I ate cereal instead of cold pizza so my breath wouldn't smell like pepperoni. Then I sat around waiting for the doorbell to ring.

Even when my mother and I were pulling out of the driveway to go to St. Luke's I was looking down the street hoping to catch sight of Tim heading toward our house on the cross country skis he uses to build up his leg muscles. I know we live miles from his house, but there was a thin layer of snow covering the ground, and he had skiied over to my house once. It was just possible he would do it again. If he really liked me. Which evidently he didn't.

On the drive to St. Luke's I thought about how Alex had told me off last Saturday. I could feel my cheeks get hot just remembering how he had called me smug and lectured me about looking down my nose at other people. This week I was going to show him a thing or two. I was going to sit with those guys and talk to them and act like I was enjoying myself.

When we got there I looked around for Alex but didn't see him. I started putting out the napkins and silverware, then helped set out the big steam trays full of food. Still Alex didn't show up. While I was serving green beans I looked up and saw him come in the door with his dad. He was wearing jeans and a gray sweatshirt with the sleeves pushed up and a down vest.

Alex came right over to me and, in front of everyone, apologized for how he had treated me the week before.

"I had no right to rail on at you like I did," he said. He didn't even whisper. He said it right out loud and I felt like everyone was looking at us.

"Would you like a megaphone so the guy at the end of the line can hear?" I whispered, dying of embarrassment. I knew my mother had heard and was probably wondering what it was all about.

"Sorry," he said, lowering his voice, "but it's been bothering me all week."

"It's okay. Just forget it," I shrugged.

After we had served the meal and cleaned up the kitchen, Alex went into the dining room and sat down with Charles and a few other guys. I took a deep breath and followed.

One of them got up and offered me his chair. Some of the others welcomed me. They called me Bashful.

I fidgeted in my chair, trying to think of something to say. Nothing came into my head so I just listened to them talk about how cold it's been. I started to wonder where they sleep and how they keep warm and where they go to the bathroom and shave and wash up.

"Hey, Alex, you heard about Stubs?" one of the men said. "He froze himself. Charles found him . . . when was it, Charles? Two, three days ago? He was laying under the Main Street bridge like he was asleep. But he was froze near to death. Tell him about it, Charles."

"Drop it, Bernie. I don't want to talk about it," Charles said and walked away. He stood near the front door looking at the swirling snow outside. Bernie pulled out a deck of cards.

"Five card stud. Who's in? You want to play, Alex?"

Alex shook his head and went over to Charles. They sat down together and talked quietly, their heads bent forward, almost touching.

I felt so bad I almost started to cry. I wondered if Stubs had died or what? I wondered where he was.

After a minute Alex went into the kitchen. I saw him talking to his father. Charles stayed where he was, his head hanging down. I went over to him and sat down in the chair Alex had just left.

"Is Stubs okay?" I asked.

"He's at City Hospital. Maybe he'll live. Maybe

he'll die. Makes no difference to me. He was just a pest, anyway. Could barely tie his shoes without my help."

"I think Stubs likes you a lot."

Charles turned and looked at me. His eyes looked scared. He looked back down at the floor and said, "Well, I don't need nobody liking me. I don't need nobody depending on me. I helped him 'cause I felt sorry for him. I used to tell him, 'Stubs, you are the sorriest creature the Lord ever put on this earth.' " Charles stopped talking and turned his head the other way. I saw his shoulders shake like he was crying.

I wanted to put my arm around him and tell him it was okay to cry. But I just couldn't bring myself to do it. I touched his hand, instead. It felt rough and chapped. I took my hand away.

"Stubs'll be all right. Don't worry," I said softly.

"God, he was so stupid to sleep under the bridge that night. I told him, 'Stubs, come on over to the shelter. It's going to hit zero tonight.' And he promised he would. He promised. Told me he just wanted to walk along the river path and pick up some empty bottles and cans to cash in. He must've stopped to rest and fallen asleep. He never came to the shelter. I looked for him. Almost missed him it was so dark under the bridge. But I found him. Ran to a store and had them call an ambulance."

Charles pulled a filthy red bandana out of his pocket and blew his nose.

"Maybe I'll play myself a little poker," he said but he didn't move, just stayed there with his head hanging down and his hands clasped between his knees. Pretty soon I saw a tear fall onto the floor in front of Charles. After a few minutes he blew his nose again and walked away. A smoky smell, like a campfire, hung in the air after he left.

I sat there with a lump in my throat, thinking about how Stubs had changed his socks in front of me the week before and how his old socks had been dirty and full of holes.

I went into the kitchen and asked Alex if Stubs was going to be all right.

"I don't know. My father went to call the hospital. He'll find out the story."

"Alex, I feel so bad for Charles. You know what I think? Charles is afraid to get close to anyone because of what he went through when he lost his wife and daughter. And he really does love Stubs but he won't admit it. I wish I could do something to help him."

"You did. You showed him you cared."

"Alex, where does Charles sleep? Where does he keep his stuff?"

"In the winter he sleeps in church basements where volunteers set up cots every night. In warm weather he usually sleeps in doorways or under the Main Street bridge. As for 'stuff,' a lot of homeless people don't have any, because they don't have any place to keep it."

"You mean they don't even have an extra pair of underwear?"

"Some of them carry everything they own on them at all times. If they own two pairs of underwear, they wear two pairs of underwear."

"Even Charles? He's not like the others."

"You think Charles is different because you know him. He's real to you, not just a face or a name."

"It's so sad. How can stuff like this be going on right here in Easton?"

"My dad travels all over the country and he says no place is immune. Big cities like New York have their own kinds of homeless problems and small places like Easton have theirs, maybe not as complex, but just as real. The bottom line is the same. There are people who don't know where they'll sleep from one day to the next."

"Why doesn't somebody do something?"

"My dad and your mom and some others are trying to get the city to donate a building where there'd be showers and cots and lockers for them, and where they could get help straightening their lives out if they want to. And they're working to get low income housing built so the poor can have permanent homes."

I looked across the kitchen at my mother. She was wrapping sandwiches in waxed paper and talking and laughing with some of the other volunteers. I got a funny feeling, like it was the first time I was looking at her and seeing somebody more than just my mom. I went over and helped her wrap sandwiches.

When Alex's father came back he told us that Stubs was alive, but barely. He said he was going to the hospital to visit him and would take any of the guys who wanted to go. We watched as Mr. Henley went to the dining room and spoke to the men. A couple of them got up to leave with him. Charles stayed in his chair.

After they left, Charles got up without a word and walked out the door into the cold, gusting wind.

Mom and I talked on the way home about Stubs and Charles and some of the other men she had come to know in the four years since she started working at St. Luke's.

"Have any of them died?"

"Of course."

"Do you feel bad when one of them dies?"

"Very."

"Is that why you're working to get better shelters and housing?"

"How did you know about that?"

"Alex told me. Mom? Why do you work at the soup kitchen?"

"I guess because I feel that all of us should care about each other and reach out to each other somehow."

"Does it make you happy?"

"Yes, but it's a different kind of happy from the way you think of the word. It's the kind of happy that comes from doing what I feel is right and good."

"Mom? I want to do something to help." Mom reached over and rubbed my arm. I turned to face her. "Just tell me what to do and I'll do it. Anything."

"Well, honey," she said. "I think you should decide what you want to do. Get some ideas and we'll talk about them."

All the way home I kept seeing Charles's red, chapped hands in my mind.

"You know what I'd like to do?" I said to my mother as we pulled in the driveway. "I'd like to take up a collection at school to buy gloves for all the people who come to St. Luke's. We could wrap the gloves and give them as Christmas presents. What do you think?"

"I think that shows you're becoming a very caring young lady." She leaned over and kissed me.

I went up to my room and pulled out my notebook from behind *The World's Greatest Classics*. I opened it to the page where I had listed my faults and virtues. I added virtue number eight: caring.

I looked into the mirror over my dresser and smiled at myself.

14 On Sunday, with a week to go before Christmas, I was so loaded with holiday spirit I decided to go with my family to cut down a Christmas tree, something I haven't done since I was nine.

I was especially happy since Mr. Henley had called that morning to tell Mom and me that Stubs wasn't going to die.

We piled into the car and drove out to the tree farm and then I realized the reason I usually stay home. My father insists on finding the *perfect* tree. Of course, the perfect tree is never right next to where we park the car. It's always a kajillion miles across the fields.

All of us took turns pointing out the perfect tree to my father, but it was no use. He had the ax and the saw and he refused to use them. He assured us he would *know* when we came upon the *perfect* tree.

It was right after Mary announced that she had to go potty . . . *bad,* that the perfect tree appeared before my father, like magic. It had a couple of bald spots and leaned a little to one side, but we all agreed that it was just the tree we had been searching for.

We tied it to the top of the car and sang Christmas carols all the way home. Mary wet her pants in the car.

I love decorating the tree. Every year we laugh at the plaster nativity-scene ornament that Joel made in first grade, which has to be hung on the bottom branch because it weighs five pounds, and the construction paper heart with a picture of me, five years old and missing my two front teeth, glued onto it. There's the gaudy pine cone rolled in sparkles that Chris made in Cub Scouts, and all the ornaments made of can lids, styrofoam egg cups, and bottle caps that my mother gets teary-eyed over.

This year was the first Mary helped decorate the tree. Every time we handed her an ornament she hung it on the same branch, till the branch was so loaded it almost touched the floor. My mother ran for the camera and took a picture.

When we finished decorating, we clicked off all the lamps and my father plugged in the tree lights. It looked beautiful. The perfect tree.

My mother made us all sit down on the couch together with our arms around each other and just look at the tree in silence.

"Hey," I said after a few minutes, "I've got this great idea. Let's all make gifts this year instead of buying them. You're always saying, Mom, how Christmas is too commercial and everybody's lost the true meaning and all that. So I was thinking, hey, let's make this Christmas meaningful and give each other stuff right from the heart."

"Broke, huh?" Joel asked.

"Totally."

Dad reached behind Mom to squeeze my shoulder. "My wallet and I vote yes to that suggestion," he said.

"Wait a minute. I'm not sure you completely understand, Dad," I explained. "Santa'll come and bring stuff for us kids. Right, Mary? We'll just make the gifts we give each other."

"Or better yet," Mom cut in, "instead of gifts, let's give each other letters saying what we love about the other person."

"Gimme a break," Joel groaned.

"Let's not get weird about this," I added.

Mom wasn't about to give up. "Okay," she said, "how about this? Instead of giving *things*, let's give each other services. Like Patty could give Joel a few days of delivering his newspapers, or Chris could offer to clean Patty's room, or Joel could give Chris backgammon lessons, things like that."

"Yeah," I jumped in. "Really, that would make Christmas special."

"And cheap," Joel added, looking directly at me.

Just then the phone rang. "It's settled then," I said as I jumped up to answer it, "we give ourselves to each other this Christmas."

"Patty, where have you been all day?" Tracy screeched into the phone the instant I said hello. "You will absolutely die when I tell you what you missed out on! You are going to hate yourself! I mean it. You're going to want to get a gun and shoot yourself when I tell you where I've been and where you could have been with me!"

"Hey," I answered, "if it's that bad, maybe you'd better not tell me."

"Jeez, Patty. Wait a minute. Let me catch my breath. I'm starting to hyperventilate. Okay. I'm okay now. Okay. Where do I start? Okay. This morning the phone rings and it's Scott and he asks me if I want to go to Benton Mountain ski lodge with him for the day. Can you believe it? He tells me that Tim is going to ask you to go too and Scott's father is going to drive all of us there. So I act like boys invite me to go skiing all the time. I tell him I think I can make it. So he tells me they'll pick me up in an hour. I call you and no answer. An hour later Tim and Scott show up. No Patty. Tim says he's been calling you but you're not home. So the three of us spend the day at the ski lodge. It was awesome. Patty, skiing is so-o-o fun!"

"What?" I yelled at the top of my lungs. "I spent all day in a freezing cold field searching for the perfect Christmas tree and rode home in a car smelling of pee when I could have been sitting around a lodge fireplace with Tim Shokow? I can't stand it! Please tell me you're kidding."

"No, I am not kidding. I would not kid you about something this awesome."

"So what happened? Tell me everything!"

"Well, to tell you the truth I hardly saw Scott all day. The two of them went right to Rocket Trail and I spent my time on the little bunny slope. I didn't see Scott till it was time to leave. But we did sit real close together coming home in the car. I'll tell you more tomorrow. I've got to go now. I still have my jacket on and I have to go to the john and I'm dead tired." She hung up before I could even say 'bye.

As I was walking away from the phone it rang again. It was Tim, calling to tell me all the fun I had missed out on.

I went back in the living room and looked at the tree again. It looked kind of crooked and the bare spot showed up like crazy. I could swear I saw a few needles fall off, too.

15 While we waited for the school bus on Monday morning, Tracy talked my ear off about her day at Benton.

"Skiing is so awesome," she said. "I think I'm going to try out for the ski team next year."

"Trace," I reminded her, "you spent the entire day on the bunny slope with the five-year olds."

"Doesn't matter," she said confidently. "I had the feeling I was born to ski." She flexed her knees and turned her body from side to side, making swishing sounds.

"Never mind about skiing. Tell me the good parts."

"Well, like I said yesterday, I hardly saw Scott all day. But the ride home made up for it. We sat real close in the back seat of Tim's father's car, and the last ten minutes, Scott held my hand."

"Did your hand get sweaty?"

"Actually I had my gloves on."

"Did Tim talk about me?"

"Tim hardly talked at all."

"I hope you found a way to bring up the subject of Patty Dillman," I said, nudging Tracy with my elbow.

"Patty who?" Tracy laughed and then added, "Of course I brought up Patty Dillman. I talked about the ski trip we'll be taking over vacation and how you can't wait to be sitting with Tim in front of a roaring fire at the lodge, with his arm around you and your head on his shoulder."

"Tracy, you didn't!"

"I didn't. What do you think I am, a birdbrain? And don't answer that or I'll put snow down your neck."

Just then the bus pulled up. On the ride to school Tracy kept yakking about her day at Benton but I hardly heard her. I got to thinking about my plan to raise money for the guys at St. Luke's, and I got to thinking that maybe it wasn't such a good idea, after all. I mean, what if nobody gave money? What if everybody laughed at me and said it was dumb? What if everybody thought I was doing it just to make points with the teachers? What if everybody thought I was a dweeb and I got a reputation and no one ever talked to me again or wanted to be my friend?

I was starting to get all nervous and clammy when Tracy punched me in the arm and said, "You're not listening, are you? What's the matter, are you feeling bad that you missed out on yesterday? Well, don't worry. In exactly one week Tim Shokow will be sitting next to you, holding your hand [Tracy took my hand in hers] and saying, 'Patricia, my darling, this is the moment I have been waiting for since the beginning of time. You are the most beautiful and ravishing girl, I mean woman, I have ever laid eyes on. May the fire that burns in me last for all eternity.' "

I yanked my hand away just as Tracy lifted it to

her mouth to kiss it. "You're sick, you know that?" I said.

After a few minutes I asked Tracy, "Do you ever get an idea that seems really great and then, after you think about it awhile, you start to think it's stupid?"

"Never."

"Well, I got this idea and now I'm thinking maybe I shouldn't go through with it." I told her about my plan to ask the kids at St. Iggie's to donate money for gloves. Tracy said it was a super idea.

"Then if I get permission to do it, would you make the announcement over the PA for me? You know how nervous I get making speeches."

"Not a chance. It was your idea. You should make the announcement and get the credit."

"Would you at least come over to the Wards' house after school to help me plan the strategy?"

"Pats, I'd love to. But look out the window. It's starting to snow. This'll be the perfect day for me to go out delivering calendars on my new paper route. And tonight I was planning on going over to Easton Valley Park to practice skiing."

"You hate the idea, don't you?"

"I love the idea."

"Look, you don't have to be polite with me. If you hate the idea, just say so. I can take it."

"I love the idea and just to prove it I'll make a deal with you. Come skiing with me tonight and I'll spend every spare minute for the rest of the week helping with your fund-raising project."

"You don't play fair."

"Yeah, I love it. Deal?"

"Every spare minute?"

"Yup."

"Day and night?"

"Yup."

"If I call you up in the middle of the night to talk about it, you will?"

"Yup."

"And you'll make the announcement over the PA?"

"Nope."

"I thought I could trick you on that one. Well, okay. It's a deal. I'll go skiing with you, but the minute I fall, I'm quitting."

Just then the bus whooshed to a stop in front of school and the door belched open. Tracy told me one more time that she loved the idea and then she got shoved ahead of me into the squeeze of kids forcing their way off the bus.

"She hates it," I said out loud.

I walked into homeroom and went directly to Sister Clarabelle's desk, before I had time to think about what I would say and end up losing my nerve.

"Could I talk to you for a minute, Sister? In private?" I asked her. We went into the back room. She sat down at the table and made a motion for me to do the same. Instead, I stood at the doorway tucking in my blouse as I blurted out, "Sister, I've got this idea I want to ask you about. You'll probably think it's stupid, and I don't blame you, but here goes." I told her about going to St. Luke's and hating it and about Stubs changing his socks at the table and about Alex telling me off and Charles crying over Stubs and about how if they own two pairs of underwear they wear them both, and about my plan to ask for donations from the kids at St. Iggie's to buy gloves for Christmas.

I finished with, "It's a dumb idea, isn't it?"

"Well," said Sister Clarabelle. "Let me think about this for a moment."

"It's okay. Never mind. Forget I ever came in here." I started to leave.

"Patricia, please sit down and kindly stop that babbling. Your idea is very kind. What I was thinking about was whether this is the kind of request that can be accommodated through the school." She stood up. "Let me look into the matter. I'll talk to you at the end of the day."

During study hall the intercom phone rang. Mrs. LaShomb mumbled something into it, then turned to the class and said, "Patricia Dillman, you're wanted at the principal's office." All the blood drained out of my face and I could feel everybody's eyes on me. The only time kids get called to the office is if they're in mega trouble. While Mrs. LaShomb filled out a pass I tried to think of every rule I'd broken lately. After a few seconds it hit me. Someone had found the pencils and my monogrammed pen stuck in the ceiling of room 212. The principal was about to grill me for the details. Then I would probably get suspended from school. Wait till I got my hands on spaghetti-brain Joyce Nesmith.

I wanted to run into the john and hide there till school let out, then sneak home and never come back to St. Iggie's, but instead I forced myself to put one foot in front of the other and walk into the principal's office. I gave my name to the secretary, then pulled up my socks and tugged down at my skirt. I tucked in my blouse and ran my hand across my mouth in case I had on too much lipstick.

"Good morning, Patricia," Sister Marianne said in a real businesslike voice, as I opened the door and took a couple of halfhearted steps into her huge office.

"Good morning, Sister," I answered, but I was thinking that it was actually a lousy morning, what with me about to get suspended and all.

"Patricia, I hear you've been involved in an interesting project."

"Well, Sister. I wouldn't exactly call it a project. It was sort of something that just kind of happened. It wasn't planned or anything. Honest. And I wasn't the one who got the idea, either. I'm not going to rat on anybody, but I just want you to know I didn't come up with the idea. I just happened to be there."

"I must have gotten incorrect information. I was told it was your idea."

"No. No way. I just sort of got involved without wanting to and my pen was the only thing with a name on it, so I'm the one who's going to take all the heat."

"Yes, I'm sure you are. But about this project, or whatever it is you want to call it, that has come to my attention. I'm sorry to say that, as much as I'd like to, I just can't permit that sort of thing. I'm sorry, you'll have to go elsewhere."

I was stunned. It had happened as simply as that. I was kicked out of St. Iggie's through no fault of my own. All because of spaghetti-brain Joyce Nesmith and my grandmother. Sister Marianne didn't even give me a chance to defend myself. She didn't care that I loved St. Iggie's and I could never be happy *elsewhere.* I could feel tears starting up so I squeezed my eyes shut to stop them. It didn't do any good.

"I'm so sorry, dear," Sister Marianne was saying. She got up and came around her desk to put her hand on my shoulder. "We have rules and guidelines that we must abide by. I can't make exceptions."

"Could . . . could I at least h-have my p-p-pen back?" I asked through hiccups. I was crying full force by now.

"I'm sorry, dear, I don't have your pen. And let me say again how sorry I am that I can't allow this idea to be carried out here. If we let one student collect money, even though it is for a very worthy cause, soon it could get out of hand. So we simply do not allow it at all. Sister Barbara Clare tried to persuade me to make an exception for you, but I couldn't. I do hope you'll be able to raise the money by some other means."

I stopped crying in mid-snuffle. I gulped and swallowed hard. I excused myself, ran out the door and barely made it to the john before I started to laugh so hysterically I got a second case of hiccups.

At dismissal Sister Clarabelle told me how sorry she was that I wouldn't be allowed to raise money at school. "Sister Marianne told me how disappointed you were. She asked me to tell you that she's proud of you. And she hopes you find your pen."

When I got to the Wards' house I set Max up with some fingerpaints and then sat down with a blank sheet of filler paper to list money-raising ideas. I was going to have my family vote on the best one at supper.

When suppertime came my paper was still blank.

So, while we ate we brainstormed trying to come up with some way to raise hundreds of dollars in the next four days. Nobody could think of anything and I was starting to get a headache so I just excused myself and left to get ready for skiing.

"I don't know why I let you talk me into this," I complained to Tracy when I got in her car.

"Jeez, if you're going to spend the entire night complaining, you may as well just go back to your house right now and not make both of us miserable."

I almost made it out the car door before she grabbed my arm and yanked me back inside.

We got to Easton Valley Park and put on our skis in the little cinderblock building that serves as a picnic lodge in the summer and a warming shelter during ski season. It was a beautiful night. The air was crisp and cold and you could see big, fat snowflakes in the bright path of the floodlights aimed at the ski slope.

It felt different from the time I was there for a lesson. This time I could relax, knowing that every goof I made wasn't being watched by a teacher and a whole class. I was wobbly every time I went up the tow rope and I fell a lot and I spent most of my downhill time doing the wedge so I could keep a manageable speed of about one mile an hour. But after a couple of hours, as Tracy and I were warming up in the shelter, I found myself wanting to get back outside to practice some more. I was enjoying skiing!

On the way home Tracy and I were totally hyper, talking about skiing. I also told her about how the money-raising plan had bombed and how I had spent hours trying to think up a new one. Tracy promised to try to come up with some new ideas, too.

When I got home I called Tim and got hyper all over again talking about skiing with him. He was so excited he kept calling me "hot dog" every three seconds. Even when I changed the subject and told him about wanting to raise money for gloves, he told me I should raise money by giving hotdogging lessons.

"Wait a minute. You just gave me an idea," I said. "I've got to hang up. Talk to you later."

"Dad!" I screeched at the top of my lungs. "Where are you?"

"He's outside stringing up the hawthorn tree with Christmas lights," Mom called from the kitchen.

Every year Mom asks him to do something a little more sophisticated with the outdoor decorating. But every year he loads up the little hawthorn tree with twenty strings of lights and thinks it's a masterpiece.

I ran outside. Joel and Chris heard my yelling and followed me out.

"Dad!" I called up into the hawthorn tree where Dad was leaning against a ladder stringing lights. "I have an idea. Remember how we worked at the hot dog booth during last summer's church picnic? Remember the hot dogs and rolls and all the other stuff were donated and the church made a bundle of money on it? Well, could we do the same thing at an Easton basketball game? Is there a game coming up in the next few days? Do you think they'd let us do it? Do you think we could get the stuff donated? Do you think we could get everything organized?"

"Hey, slow down," Dad said as he climbed down the ladder and sat on the bottom rung. "I think you might just have something there. This Thursday's basketball game is against our arch-rival Edinburg. There's always a full house for that game. But let's not get all excited till I find out if we'd be allowed to sell hot dogs."

"Hey," piped in Joel, "we could call it Halftime Hot Dogs For the Homeless." I turned to Joel and gave him a dirty look.

"Sorry," he said. "I got carried away."

I was excited, too. "Dad, do you really think this can work?"

"It's possible, but let's not even think about the details till we get permission from Easton. I'll look into it tomorrow."

"Let's go inside and make a list of everything that needs to get done," Joel said to me.

"Can I help?" Chris wanted to know. "Maybe me and my friends can make posters. Could we, huh?"

"Sure," I said. "And thanks everyone. This is going to be great."

Dad laughed as he climbed back up the ladder. "It's nice to know that you're all taking my advice and not moving ahead till I get the official okay."

16 The next night Dad came home from work with the good news that we could use halftime at Thursday's game for our fund-raising project.

After supper Chris called a bunch of friends to come over and make posters. Joel and I sat down with a stack of filler paper and started making lists.

Joel is so organized. He started with a two-column list called Things To Do and Who'll Do Them. Underneath we wrote:

1. Get permission — Dad
2. Call to get stuff donated — Patty
3. Pick up donated staff — Mom, Chris
4. Get volunteers — Joel, Patty
5. Set up
6. Sell hotdogs
7. Clean up
8. Publicity — make and hand out flyers before game — Joel
9. Get money box and rolls of coins to make change

Then he made a list called Things We Need
Donated. Under that we listed:

Item	Quantity
1. Hot dogs	
2. Rolls	
3. Mustard, ketchup, relish	
4. Napkins	
5. Grill	

We figured we could fill out the second column
later.

His third list was called Volunteers and we listed
our family's names. We agreed that the next day we
would ask all our friends to volunteer.

Every time we had a question for Dad we had to
go to the front door and yell it outside. Dad was on
a ladder propped against the hawthorn tree again,
stringing up more Christmas lights.

"How many people will be at the game?" I yelled
out the door. "How many hot dogs do you think
we can sell?" Joel yelled a few minutes later. "How
much should we charge?" I hollered at the hawthorn tree, which by now had begun to twinkle on
and off.

"Thanks, Joel. I really appreciate this," I said as
we finished and he put the lists into a file folder.
"You know, someday I've got to show you the list

I made about your faults and virtues like it said to do in that Teenspeak column you read me." His face got all red and he got up and left the room.

Chris and his friends had just finished doing their artwork and came marching into the kitchen as Joel walked out. They shoved him back in and made the whole family take seats around the table while they held up the four posters they had made.

Each one said "Halftime Hot Dogs For the Homless," with homeless spelled wrong. They had decorated the posters with drawings of stuff like hot dogs and bottles of ketchup. The posters were so bad they were funny. But we clapped after each one was held up.

After his friends had left I went up to Chris's room and asked him why he and his friends had taken turns all evening coming into the kitchen and giggling at me.

"I can't tell," he said.

"Look, I didn't want to make a scene in front of your friends and embarrass you, but you guys were laughing at me, Chris, and I want to know why."

"I can't tell."

"You better tell or I'll turn all your baseball cards into confetti."

"You'll never find them, so there, wienie head."

I walked over to his closet. He didn't move. I walked over to his dresser. He didn't budge. I walked over to his toybox. He stood like a statue. I walked toward his bed and he got hysterical.

"Okay, okay, I'll tell. I'll tell. But don't get mad." So he told me that he and his friends have a club and one of the rules is that every time you have a meeting you have to tell the other members a secret. A good secret. So he had told his friends that he saw me kissing Tim the night Tim came over to give me a ski lesson. Evidently that qualified as a "good secret" and warranted hysterical giggling.

"You were spying on us! You little . . ." I started to say as I lunged for him.

Chris ran into the bathroom and locked the door.

"Worm," I yelled, pounding at the door.

"Wienie head," he yelled back.

"Do I have to come up there?" Mom yelled from the bottom of the stairs.

"Someday soon, Chris," I said slowly and menacingly to the bathroom door, "you are going to wake up in the morning and go into the bathroom and look in the mirror and see that during the night someone has shaved your head. And no one will ever know for sure, except you and me, who did it. After that, you'll look like a bowling ball with legs for about three months. Then your hair will start to sprout in little blond spikes that hardly show. Pretty soon the spikes will stick straight out, no matter how you try to plaster them down. All the girls will laugh at you. No one will want to be caught dead in your company. You'll spend all your time in the bathroom putting Vaseline on your hair to keep it down. In the end you'll run away from home and join a circus. Then, and only then, will I have some peace in my life."

"I'm going to tell Mom and Dad right now what you said. Then when it happens they'll know you did it."

"I really don't care. Even if I get grounded for a year it'll be worth it." I gave the bathroom door a smack with the flat of my hand and walked away.

"Big, fat, double wienie head," Chris shouted after me.

Tim called later that night to tell me that he had made the school ski team.

"Great," I said halfheartedly. I was remembering how football had completely taken over his life in the fall, only it hadn't bothered me too much then because I was involved with the school play. Now skiing was doing the same thing to him in the winter. I wondered what sport he would get addicted to in the spring.

"Do you play tennis?" I asked him.

"No, do you?"

"No. What are your feelings on baseball?"

"I like the Red Sox. Why?"

"No reason. By the way, do you run, high jump, pole vault, or throw shot put?"

"No."

"Good. Now that that's cleared up, can I change the subject and ask you a favor? Could you help me out with our fund raising project? We're selling hot dogs during Thursday's Easton basketball game. Maybe you could come?"

"I'd really like to, Patty, but I can't. Ski team," he said. Then he told me about all the ski-team competitions that were coming up. During the rest of our conversation I flipped through the December issue of *Junior Miss* magazine that happened to be on the hall table.

As I was getting ready for bed that night my mother came in and made me go tell Chris I was just kidding about shaving his head.

17

Day: Thursday, December 22.
Time: 6:30 P.M.
Place: Easton College Gym

Everything had gone like clockwork. Mom had told me a few places to call for donations. She said that some businesses were willing to give their products to charitable causes they believed in and use the donations as tax write-offs.

So I had made a few calls and explained my project to everyone from the receptionist to the general manager and gotten donations of one hundred pounds of hot dogs (translation: seven hundred hot dogs) from a local meat-packing company, giant dispensers of mustard and ketchup from a restaurant supply warehouse, and rolls from the distribution center of Easton's biggest supermarket chain. The meat-packing company had even made arrangements for two giant grills and warming ovens to be delivered to the gym.

Joel had made a flyer advertising:

> BUY A HOTDOG
> DURING HALFTIME
>
> PROCEEDS WILL BE USED
>   TO AID THE HOMELESS
> DURING THIS HOLIDAY SEASON

Dad had taken the flyer to work and made one thousand copies. I had come home from school and used up a whole box of tissues chopping onions. And we had recruited twenty volunteers from among my friends, Joel's friends, and the workers at St. Luke's Kitchen. When I had asked at the lunch table, Whitney, Kate, Tracy, Jeannie, and Trish had all volunteered to come. Only Allison couldn't make it because she was in some kind of gymnastics competition.

Now, one hour before game time, the volunteers were milling in the hall outside the gym, while Joel walked around with a clipboard telling people what their jobs were.

"Who's the hunk?" Tracy asked when Joel gave Alex the job of handing out flyers with me at one of the gym entrances.

"A guy who helps out at St. Luke's," I explained.

"So how come you haven't told me about him? Saving him all for yourself?" She poked me in the arm.

"No, he's just a nice guy, a friend. In case you've forgotten I happen to be in love with Tim," I said as I grabbed a stack of flyers from Joel.

Dad and Alex's father were already busy cooking hot dogs and putting them into the ovens to keep warm. It was going to be a zoo the minute the half-time buzzer sounded. We were going to have to move seven hundred hot dogs in twenty minutes.

I had a mega case of stomach butterflies. But when the half-time buzzer rang things got so hectic there wasn't time to be nervous. People swarmed around the two long tables in the hall that served as counters. The crowd was seven and eight people deep and I frantically handed out hot dogs till the buzzer sounded again, signalling that the second half was about to start.

We all collapsed into folding chairs while Dad and Mr. Henley counted the leftover hot dogs. Then Dad stood on a chair and said, "Could I have everyone's attention? It looks like we've made about six hundred fifty dollars. Congratulations everyone." We all let out a loud cheer. People slapped me on the back and hugged me. It felt great.

Since it was a week night, most of the volunteers went right home. My dad, Mr. Henley, Alex, and I stayed to clean up. Alex and I went into the gym to pick up all the discarded flyers and stuff them into a giant trash barrel on wheels. After we had finished we sat down on the top bleacher and leaned back against the wall. I was so tired I could hardly keep my eyes open, but I knew I wouldn't sleep much that night. Inside I was still pumped up from the excitement of the sale.

"You must be awfully pleased," Alex said.

"I am. I really am," I answered and sighed with satisfaction.

Alex took off his baseball hat, put it on my head and said, "I hereby crown you queen of the hot dogs. Long live the queen."

"Wow! Queen of the hot dogs. Eat your heart out Princess Di."

I stood up and turned toward the empty bleachers below me. "Thank you all for this great honor," I said in a loud voice. "I have worked toward this moment and dreamed of this moment all my life. I promise always to uphold the dignity of my office and my title. As long as I live I shall work tirelessly to spread the good news of the hot dog to every corner of this land. And when I die I ask only that I be buried with a hot dog in my hand, ketchup, no relish, and a message over my tomb: 'Here lies the world's greatest wienie head.' Thank you my loyal subjects. You may now bow before me."

Alex bowed. I put his hat back on his head and sat down. "How come you always wear this?" I asked him.

Alex fingered the letters on the hat. "It's from my brother. He's serving on the submarine *Parche* right now and the hat kind of keeps him close to me even though he's far away. It's funny. My father is so much against war and nuclear weapons and then one of his sons goes off and enlists and ends up on a battle submarine. I guess kids don't always turn out like their parents want them to."

"Yeah, like me. I spend most of my life getting into trouble and not being the model kid my parents wish I was. But you're different. I bet your parents are proud of you."

"Yeah, sometimes," Alex said. Then he turned to

me and grinned. "Are you aware that you smell like a hot dog?"

"Are you aware that you've got mustard on your face?" I answered and wiped it off with the corner of my apron.

Someone flicked off the lights in the gym. Alex and I sat there in the dark for a while, not saying anything. It felt nice sitting there with him. Not heart pounding nice like with Tim, but just comfortable, like you feel when you're with a friend. After a few minutes we climbed down the bleachers and out of the darkened gym.

18 Mom made a list of places for me to call—places that might have lots of gloves available. I made the calls during Friday's lunch hour and lucked out. I located a stockpile of gloves at a wholesale warehouse that sells stuff to businesses. So Mom picked me up from school and we drove directly to the place. Luckily I didn't have to baby-sit Max and the twins because Easton College had started its Christmas break.

The warehouse was a huge building jam packed with stacks of brown packing boxes. It echoed with the whirring sounds of forklifts and men yelling to each other. The manager was short and chubby with a soggy cigar clamped in the corner of his mouth. Even though it was freezing cold in there, he wore only slacks and a short-sleeved shirt with about a dozen pens clipped to the front pocket.

"Yeah, I remember you," he said when I introduced myself, "and you're in luck. I got enough gloves for an army." He kept the cigar in his mouth while he talked. I couldn't help staring at it as it bobbed up and down.

He led us through a maze of aisles piled high on each side with boxes. He stopped in front of one box that looked just like all the others, jabbed a hole in it with his pocket knife and ripped the hole big enough so he could reach inside. He pulled out a pair of black knit gloves. A few boxes farther down the aisle, he did the same thing and pulled out a gaudy pair of orange leather gloves.

"You got two choices," he said. "You got these knit jobs that I got comin' outta my ears. I got enough of these babies for an army. They're cheap and that's just what they are: cheap. They wouldn't keep your hands warm if you was holdin' a hot coal inside of 'em.

"Then I got these orange babies. Some hotsy-totsy designer in New York decided the 'in' color for gloves was gonna be orange. As you can tell by my inventory stacked up to the ceiling, she was wrong. And I hope to hell, excuse my French, that she got canned before she could dream up any more God-awful color schemes. These orange babies are ugly as sin, but they're leather and they're warm. See this here lining? Them government scientists come up with this for the space program. You could be standin' on a streetcorner on Mars in the dead of winter and your fingers'd stay toasty.

"I can sell you either of these babies cheap. The knits are two bucks apiece. The gaudy ones are three. Either way you go, I ain't making diddly squat on 'em. Just wanna move 'em outta here."

"What do you think, Mom?" I asked. I knew we had only six hundred fifty dollars to spend. Mom took both pairs of gloves and tried them on. The black ones did look kind of thin and the orange ones did look kind of ugly. Mom took forever feeling them and inspecting every inch of them.

"We'll take two hundred fifty pairs of the orange gloves if you can give them to us for two-fifty apiece," Mom offered.

"Look, lady, I know this is for a good cause, so I already gave you my rock-bottom price. I'd give 'em to you free if it was up to me. Like I said, I ain't making diddly squat on 'em. These gloves go for thirteen, fourteen bucks retail. I ain't planning no trip to Disneyworld on the profits, believe me."

Mom put down the orange gloves and started to look more closely at the black ones. "These are the only two styles you have?"

"If you need that many, yeah, those are your choices."

I took a black glove from my mother and put it on. I could see my skin through the thin knit. I thought of Charles' coarse, red hands and of Stubs freezing under a bridge. I thought about how cold my hands get when the school bus is a few minutes late. My hand went down to my side and touched my purse where the ski trip money was tucked inside my wallet. I had the fifty dollars advance Christmas present from my parents, fifty dollars from babysitting, and all the money from my bank account, plus my allowance from the past three weeks.

I shifted from one foot to the other. I stuck my hands in my pockets to warm them up. I thought about Charles' chapped hands again. I thought about Tim and the ski trip. I wondered how I would ever explain it to him if I gave some of my money for the gloves. I wondered if Tracy would be mad.

It seemed like an eternity went by as I stood there holding my hand against my purse. My hand started to feel like it was on fire. Finally I said, "Oh my gosh, I almost forgot. Some people at school heard about the project and made donations today." I tried to sound convincing.

As I reached into my purse and fumbled for my wallet, I went on, "Things have been so hectic I completely forgot about it." I flipped through my ski-trip money and pulled out five twenty-dollar bills.

"We'll take the orange gloves," Mom said, after she had counted the money I handed her. "Give us mostly large sizes, but a few smalls for the women. I believe the bill comes to seven hundred fifty dollars?"

"On the button. You got a tax-free number?"

Mom fished out a paper from her purse and handed it to the manager. We followed him to his office where he made out a receipt. Then he called someone on the intercom to carry the gloves to our car. He shook Mom's hand and we left.

The instant we got in the car Mom started railing on me. "Patty, how could you forget one hundred dollars? Do you know how that looked? It looked like we had it all planned." Just then a man came out with the gloves. Mom turned away from me and looked straight ahead till the gloves were in the trunk. Without a word, she drove to the rec center where I was supposed to turn in my ski-trip money before five P.M.

When she pulled up to the front entrance I jumped out of the car and ran inside. I stood in the hall for a few minutes, trying not to cry.

I didn't want to tell Mom what I had done. I knew she'd want to loan me the money and I knew I'd want to take it. But I had made a decision and I would follow through with it. I stood there till I got control of the tears that were trying to force their way out of my eyes. Then I went back to the car.

"Finished so fast?" Mom asked.

"Yeah, finished so fast."

"Did you make sure to get a receipt?"

"Everything's taken care of."

"I'm sorry I jumped on you, Patty. It's just that I was so embarrassed imagining what the warehouse manager thought of us. But that shouldn't matter. What matters is that we got the warmer gloves." She reached over and squeezed my shoulder.

The tears I'd been fighting forced their way behind my eyelids and I squeezed my eyes shut. I was so mixed up. I thought that if you did something noble you should feel sort of noble. You should feel all warm and special inside. But I wasn't feeling anything like that. I was starting to feel sorry for myself. I wanted to go on the ski trip so badly.

All the way home I recited the Gettysburg Address inside my head to keep my mind busy so I wouldn't cry.

That night I went to my ski lesson. I made it all the way down the hill twice without falling. Tracy kept calling me "hot dog" and goofing around and trying to get me in a good mood. I felt terrible.

"What's wrong, Patty?"

"I guess I'm just tired," I lied.

When the lesson was over my dad was waiting for us at the parking lot. We drove to Tracy's house and as we slowed to a stop at her curb she asked Dad if I could come in for a minute so she could show me something.

"What do you want to show me?" I asked when we got up to her room.

"This." Tracy made a fist and held it up to my face. "Something is wrong and I want you to tell me what it is or I'll bust your chops." Then she added softly, "Unless it's private."

I sat down on the bed and told her about the glove money.

"I ruined everything," I said. "All these weeks of planning and lessons, ruined. All my chances with Tim, ruined. My entire future, ruined. And you're probably ticked at me, too. I don't know why I did it, Tracy. I really wanted to go on that trip, especially now that I found out how much fun skiing is."

Tracy sat down next to me and started twirling

her braid. We both let out a long sigh at the same time.

"Look, I know how you feel," she said. "Remember in fifth grade when they asked for volunteers to go visit people at West Woods Nursing Home? Remember how my hand shot up in the air before anyone else's? I thought I was being a big deal by volunteering. I thought I would feel like a saint or something, but I didn't. When I started going I hated it. The patient they assigned me to kept calling me Linda and told the same stories over and over. The good feeling came, but it took a while to happen. Believe me, Patty, I know how you feel right now."

"But why did I do it, Trace? Why did I blow everything?"

"Jeez, Patty, don't ask me that. I have enough trouble figuring out why *I* do half the things I do."

"Tell me I did the right thing."

"I wish I could. But I keep thinking about the ski trip. I wish you could be there. I'm gonna miss you on that trip. Oh darn, I shouldn't be saying that. You feel bad enough already."

"It's okay," I said. "I hope you miss me. Wait a minute, I shouldn't be saying that either."

We sat for a few minutes not talking. Then Tracy said, "I take it you didn't tell Tim yet."

"Not yet."

"When are you going to?"

"I keep hoping the world will end before I have to tell him."

"I don't think it will, Pats."

"He's coming over tomorrow night with a Christmas present. I'll tell him then."

"Tell him after he gives you the present," Tracy said, and we both laughed half-heartedly.

Dad beeped lightly on the car horn. I got up to leave.

"Wait a minute," Tracy said, going to her desk and digging around in her backpack. "Speaking of presents, Mrs. Gester from the office stopped me as I was leaving school today. Asked me to give you this. She said you left before she could catch you."

I opened the small package wrapped in red tissue. Inside was my Cross pen, the one with my name inscribed on it. A card in the box read: "Patricia—The custodian found this. He wouldn't tell me where and perhaps it's best that I don't know. I'm sure you'll be happy to have it back. A blessed Christmas to you!—Sister Marianne."

"Well, that's one less thing I have to worry about," I said as I heard the car horn beep again, this time a little louder.

All the way home Dad sang Christmas carols while I chewed on my nails worrying about how to tell Tim. Even the sight of our hawthorn tree blinking its gaudy lights on and off didn't make me feel any better.

19 On Saturday, Christmas Eve, the six of us Dillmans wrapped gloves. Well, actually five of us wrapped while Mary handed us Scotch tape in foot-long strips. The job took three hours and six rolls of Scotch tape, and by the time we finished, our fingers were so stiff we could hardly bend them. Dad and Joel put the gloves in the car trunk so they'd be all ready to go on Christmas Day.

Then I made my gifts. I had bought each member of my family a Christmas card. Inside Mary's I wrote: My gift to you is two games of Hungry, Hungry Hippos every week for a year. Then I drew a picture of Mary and me playing the game together.

Inside Chris's, I promised that for one year I wouldn't make fun of anything he made in Cub Scouts or threaten to destroy his baseball card collection. I also promised I would never shave his head while he slept.

I gave Joel five days of doing his paper route for him at no charge.

For my parents I made a bunch of coupons out of index cards, that they could redeem all year long. My father's coupons listed a driveway shoveling, a lawn raking, a car washing, a grass cutting, and three "Patty's special" back rubs. My mother's coupons had a dinner preparation, a kitchen floor washing, a Dillman-secret-recipe-chocolate-zucchini cake, three hours of garden weeding, and a breakfast in bed.

I put the coupons inside their card along with a note:

Dear Mom and Dad —

I love you both very much. Even when I'm being obnoxious or doing something stupid or making you angry, please remember that I love you always, no matter what.

Love,
Patty

I sealed all the cards and put them under the tree.

Then I wrapped Tim's present, a knit neck warmer for skiing. I didn't have a gift for Tracy. She and I decided not to give each other gifts this year because of the ski trip.

I spent the rest of the day baking Christmas cookies for St. Luke's and practicing how to tell Tim my bad news.

When he came over that night we sat on the couch next to the Christmas tree and opened our gifts. His present to me was a ski hat with a huge pom-pom on top. A hot pink one.

"That's so I can spot you on the slopes next week," he said, grinning. "I can't wait for Monday, can you? It's going to be so awesome." He jammed the hat on my head so it almost covered my eyes.

I figured it was now or never.

"Tim," I said. "About the trip. I won't be going."

"Won't be going? What do you mean, you won't be going?"

I started to talk fast, trying to get all the words out without having to stop to take a breath. I couldn't bring myself to look at Tim's face so I talked into my hands, folded in my lap.

"I gave my ski trip money to the glove fund for the homeless. See, the black gloves were too thin and the warm gloves were three dollars and the guy wasn't making diddly squat and I had my ski trip money in my purse and Charles's hands are always so red and chapped and . . ."

Tim cut in. "Why didn't you just buy Charles a pair of gloves? Why did you have to blow all the money you saved?" He stopped for a minute then took my chin in his hands, turned my face toward his, and asked, "Why did you have to ruin our trip?"

"I didn't mean to. I wanted to go so badly. I wanted us to spend time together and this would have been the perfect way because you love skiing so much." I wished he would let go of my face so

I could look anywhere but at his sad eyes. My heart was pounding, every pore of my body was sweating and my scalp was prickling. The ski hat didn't help either.

"You like skiing too, don't you?"

"I do now. But I didn't when Tracy and I suggested the trip. I took lessons and rented skis and planned the trip because of you. I did it because I could see that you were more interested in skiing than in me." I stopped and took a deep breath, then finished, "I did it so I wouldn't lose you." I couldn't bring myself to look at Tim so I stared over his shoulder at the tree lights, blurring in front of my eyes.

Tim finally let go of my chin. He took the ski hat off my head. "If you wanted to go so badly, why didn't you borrow the money? I'll bet your parents would have loaned it to you."

"I wanted to, believe me. But I just couldn't. I made a decision and I had to see it through or it wouldn't have meant anything."

"But our trip didn't mean anything?"

I was getting all confused now. It wasn't going like it was supposed to, not like it had in the speeches I'd practiced all day. I picked up the wrapping paper lying on the couch between us and started twisting it around and around.

"Yes, it meant a lot. It meant making things right between us, because we'd be sharing skiing and that's your real love. That's what you really care about, more than anything else."

"I do not."

"Yes, Tim, you do." I hoped he wasn't noticing my tears plopping down on the wrapping paper. "But it's okay," I went on. "Maybe you're not ready for a steady girlfriend yet."

I wanted Tim to tell me I was wrong. I wanted him to apologize for ignoring me, and tell me I was the most important thing in his life, and that he was proud of what I had done. I wanted him to say that if I wasn't going, then he wasn't going either. I wanted him to put his arms around me and stroke my hair.

Instead he said, "I guess we've both hurt each other. Maybe we need time to think everything over. How about if we just back off for a while, okay?"

My head felt light. I grabbed the arm of the couch and held it tight. I nodded my head dumbly. "Okay."

Tim took my chin and lifted my head up. He kissed me lightly on the lips. Then he got up and left. I couldn't move to walk him to the door. I just sat there watching his broad shoulders and the way his hair curls up at the back of his neck.

I sat without moving till I heard his parents' car pull up in the driveway.

Mom stuck her head into the living room doorway, so I quickly bent down and fumbled with my sneaker laces.

"Anything wrong?" she asked.

"No," I mumbled, keeping my head bent down.

She came in and sat down next to me on the couch.

"Are you sure?"

"Yeah."

I could tell Mom had no intention of leaving so I got up and started checking the Christmas tree for blown light bulbs. Mom made small talk while I tried to swallow my sobs and get my breathing back under control.

After a few minutes I said, "Oh, did I tell you? I changed my mind about going on the ski trip." I hoped I sounded casual.

There was a long silence before Mom asked me why.

"I just don't feel like going."

"Does it have anything to do with Tim?"

"No."

"Is everything okay between you two?"

"Why shouldn't it be?"

"Want to talk about it?"

"There's nothing to talk about. I just changed my mind about going, that's all."

Before Mom could ask me any more questions I walked out and went to my room to finish crying. I cried so hard the bed shook. I had given up so much and no one even cared. Tim had talked about me hurting him, when I was the one who was hurting more than anyone. I wished I had never heard of St. Luke's. I wished no one had ever invented stupid skiing.

. . .

The next morning when I woke up I still had my clothes on. My face was ridged from the pattern in my bedspread. I felt like I hadn't slept at all. I went downstairs to join the family, determined to act like nothing was wrong. This was Christmas, the happiest day of the year.

When Mom opened my letter I got all red in the face. I sat on the floor tracing circles in the carpet while she and Dad read it. When they finished, they didn't make a big deal. Mom got up and left the room. As she walked by me, she reached down and brushed my cheek with the back of her hand.

Dad looked like he didn't know what to do so he stood up and announced, "Okay, clean up this mess and let's get the show on the road. We are not and I repeat, not, going to waltz into church late on Christmas. Understood?"

We all saluted and started shoveling wrapping paper into plastic garbage bags.

We were only about five minutes late for church.

Afterward we went right to St. Luke's to help with the big Christmas dinner. Our whole family went so we could have Christmas dinner together after the work was done. There were turkeys again, just like on Thanksgiving. And the hall was decorated. Someone had put candles and sprigs of holly on the long tables. There was a Christmas tree, and garlands of greenery draped along the serving table.

As the people drifted in, one of the volunteers sat

down at the old upright piano in the corner and played Christmas carols. I kept my eyes on the door, waiting to see Charles. I wanted to wish him a Merry Christmas.

When it came time for dinner he still hadn't arrived.

"Will he come?" I asked Alex.

"I have no idea. You never know with these guys."

The guests lined up and took their plates. They got their food and each received a pair of wrapped gloves. They ate their dinner. Still Charles hadn't arrived. I started to get nervous wondering if he had frozen under a bridge or if he had gotten into some kind of accident or if he had gotten sick.

We were eating dessert when the front door opened, letting in a cold blast of air, and Charles walked in. He was caked with ice and snow from his hatless head down to his feet. There were clumps of snow clinging to his eyebrows and his hair. I jumped out of my chair and ran over to him.

"I was so worried about you," I said, as I took his hands and peeled off the frozen-stiff, cotton gardening gloves he wore. I pulled off his coat and scraped the snow from his hair.

"Where have you been?" I asked as I led him to a place at our table. He looked at me with a puzzled expression on his face. "I went to the hospital to visit Stubs. Wanted to wish the sorry creature a Merry Christmas."

"You walked here all the way from City Hospital?" Alex asked, astonished. "That's got to be at least ten miles."

"I had nothing better to do. And I wasn't in the mood to rent a limo." Charles laughed as he sat down to his meal.

By the time he got to his dessert, the others had finished eating, so I sat with him instead of getting up to do the dishes.

"Were you really worried about me like you said?" he asked, looking at his slice of apple pie.

"Um-hm."

"Why?"

"Because I wanted to see you. I wanted to wish you a Merry Christmas and give you this." I laid a small box wrapped in red and white striped paper next to his plate. He looked at it but didn't touch it.

"Go ahead, open it. It's just something little," I urged him.

"I didn't get you a present."

"So? It's no big deal. Open it."

Charles put his fork down and wiped his hands on his pants. He unwrapped the gift like the paper was made of gold or something. I was glad Mary hadn't cut the tape for this gift or it would have taken him an hour just to loosen it. He ran his finger under each piece of tape and unfolded the ends of the paper. After it was off, he smoothed it down and folded it. Then he put the paper in his pocket. He lifted the lid of the box so slowly I wanted to scream.

"Aw, Bashful. What did you go and do this for?" he said as he lifted a little magnetic chess game from the box. "You shouldn't of done this." He took out his dirty bandana and blew his nose. "Musta caught myself a cold out there," he said and stuffed the bandana back in his pocket.

"You shouldn't of done this, really," he repeated. "I don't know what to say." Charles fingered each little chess piece. He set up the board and just stared at it for a while.

"You play?" he asked me.

"No. I never learned how."

"Too bad. It's a great game." He put the pieces back inside the folding chess board and snapped it shut. He laid it next to his plate and went back to eating his pie.

After he finished eating, he put on his orange gloves. "Nifty color," he said. "Real leather." He turned his hands over and then back. "I like 'em," he decided. Then he wore them for the rest of the afternoon.

When I stood up from Charles's table to go help clean up the kitchen, he touched my hand with his orange-gloved one. "You know," he said, looking up at me with his icy blue eyes, "I had a daughter once. She would of been about your age."

I bent down and hugged him. "Merry Christmas, Charles."

A lump formed in my throat about the size of a basketball. I went into the kitchen and started drying the dishes Alex had just washed.

"Hey, what are you trying to do, rub the pattern right off that dish?" he asked.

I smiled, but I still couldn't talk around the lump in my throat so I picked up another dish and started drying it.

"Come here," Alex said, as he took the dish and the towel from me. "I've got something for you." He took a present out of his jacket pocket and handed it to me.

"Darn. I didn't get you anything."

"Don't get too excited till you open it," he laughed.

I ripped the paper off and burst out laughing. The gift was a trophy. On a square wooden base stood a plastic hot dog in a roll, all spray-painted gold. On the base it said: "Patty Dillman, Hot Dog Queen."

"I love it. I love it. Do you realize this is my first trophy ever, other than the good-sport trophy I got for showing up every week in a bowling league in fourth grade?"

Impulsively, I gave Alex a hug and we went back to the sink. As we finished drying the dishes we could hear "Silent Night" being played softly and very sadly on a harmonica.

Pretty soon the people in the dining room started to break up, and drift outside in ones and twos and small groups. I watched them. Each one wore a pair of bright orange gloves.

Charles poked his head into the kitchen and asked if he could take a pair of gloves for Stubs.

"And thank Santy Claus for them, if you happen on him. Tell him . . . well, don't tell him anything. I think he already knows."

" 'Bye Charles," I said, as the door swung shut behind him. I pushed the door open and called out to him, "See you next week."

And then it dawned on me what I had done. Ever since Friday I'd been trying to figure it all out. And I finally knew. It was what Alex talked about and what Sister Clarabelle'd been talking about for the past month. Maybe for the first time in my life, I had done a corporal work of mercy; in the real world; from my heart.

When we got home, I put my hot-dog trophy on the mantel, next to Joel's two debating awards and his three baseball trophies.

20 Sometimes when I go to bed with something on my mind, I wake up with it all figured out. I got up on Monday knowing I had to talk to Tim before he left. So I asked Dad to drive me to the Rec Center to say good-bye to the kids going on the ski trip.

When we pulled up in front of the place there were bunches of kids standing in the doorway and all over the snow-blanketed front lawn. There were piles of duffel bags, skis, and boots all over the place and everyone was talking and laughing. You could feel the excitement in the air. I almost started crying the minute we pulled into the parking lot, but I took a deep breath and got out of the car.

Tim spotted me and right away started fumbling around with his gym bag, pretending to be looking for something. I walked up to him.

"I need to talk to you," I said. I took his arm and steered him over to the guard rail along the edge of the parking lot. We both sat down on it. Tim looked nervous and uncomfortable.

"Tim, I owe you an apology. The other day I acted like everything was your fault, but it wasn't. I chose to use my money for gloves and not go on the trip and then I expected you to feel sorry for me. It took me a while to see your side, but you were right. We both hurt each other. I'm sorry."

This time it was Tim's turn to look down and talk to his hands. "I'm sorry, too."

I touched his shoulder. "I hope you have a good time at Benton, and Merry Christmas."

"Merry Christmas to you too, Patty. And thanks." Tim smiled. He looked relieved as he got up and walked away.

I sat on the guard rail watching him, till Tracy came over and sat next to me.

"Did you tell him?" she asked.

"Um-hm."

"How'd it go?"

"Well, it went okay, unless you count the part where we broke up."

"Oh, shoot," she said, pounding the guard rail with her fist. "Look, I'm not going on the trip. I'm staying here with you." Tracy stood up and put her hands on my shoulders.

"Hold it," I said. "I feel bad enough already. Please don't make me feel like I spoiled Scott's and your trip on top of it all. Please?"

"I guess you're right. But heck I feel bad. If only you could have come, everything would have been all right."

"No, it wouldn't have. It really wouldn't have. I guess deep down I already felt that. Maybe that's why I gave up my money for the gloves."

"Are you sure you don't want me to stay?"

Tracy asked again. "We can hang out at the mall and rent *Friday The Thirteenth: Part Ninety-Three,* and dye our hair purple. It'll be fun."

I smiled. "No, you go. I'll be okay."

"Really?"

"Really."

"You sure you can handle this?"

"I'm sure."

I gave Tracy a Hershey's Kiss and a quick hug. She got on the bus and it slowly pulled away. As it turned out of the parking lot I could see Tim watching me out of one window and Tracy looking at me out of another. Gary Holmes had opened his window and was leaning out, blowing me kisses. I waved and got into Dad's car.

As soon as the front door of our house slammed behind me, Mom called out from the kitchen, "You okay?"

"Fine," I said and went up to my room. I laid on the bed for a long time, looking at a crack in the ceiling. I didn't go downstairs for lunch. I just kept staring at the ceiling.

Finally I got up and started to write my religion paper. I was sitting at my desk when Mom knocked softly and came in. She sat down on my bed.

"So," she sighed, slowly smoothing out the wrinkles in my bedspread as she talked, "they left without you. How do you feel?"

"I'll survive. But this vacation is going to be the

pits, I guarantee it. Just about every other kid on the planet earth is away someplace for vacation. Kate's at her grandmother's in Rochester. Trish is in Florida getting a tan. Tim's skiing. Tracy's skiing. Even Gary Holmes is skiing."

"Well, don't decide ahead of time that you're going to have a miserable week."

"Get real, Mom. Look at me. It's the first day of vacation and I'm sitting here with nothing better to do than start on my religion term paper."

"All I'm saying is don't pre-judge. The vacation just might turn out to be great."

"Yeah, right. Look, Mom, I'll bet you a triple scoop, pig-out special sundae at Iggie's Ice Cream Heaven that this vacation will be the most awful period of time in the history of civilization."

"It's a bet."

Mom got up to leave, but stopped at the door and turned to me. "I know you don't want to talk about it," she said, "but I have a feeling your ski-trip cancellation had something to do with the extra glove money you found in your wallet. Patty, all you had to do was ask, and Dad and I would have loaned you the money for the trip. We would have been happy, knowing what a good cause your money went to."

"I know. But I didn't want to ask. It would have made my giving the money worthless. It would have taken all the meaning out of it. I had to do it this way."

Mom came over to my desk and kissed the top of my head. "I do love you, Patty." Before I could say anything she left the room.

I got out a bunch of filler paper and was just starting on the introduction when I heard the phone ring.

Joel yelled up, "Patty, for you."

I ran downstairs and grabbed the phone, while Joel stood leaning against the wall, listening.

"Hello?"

"Hi, Patty. It's Alex. You busy?"

"No, just writing my religion paper so Joel can start typing it since he doesn't seem to have anything better to do." I glared at Joel but he didn't get the message to scram.

"Hold on a minute, will you, Alex?" I took the phone into the hall closet.

"Okay, I'm back."

"I was just wondering, if you're not too busy today, would you like a chess lesson?"

"Who's the teacher?"

"A chess master I happen to know very well."

"Does he wear a baseball hat with the words 'USS Parche' on it?"

"As a matter of fact, yes."

"And does this chess master realize that he'll be teaching the Queen of the Hot Dogs?"

"As a matter of fact he does."

"Does he know that he'll have to bow and kiss her hand and let her win every game?"

"Yes. And he's prepared to go to Ben's afterward to share a royal burger and fries."

"Then he can have an audience with Queen Patricia in one hour."

"Great. See you then."

As I ran up the stairs two at a time to fix my hair, I yelled at the top of my lungs, so Mom would hear me wherever she was, "Bet's off!"

SUSAN WOJCIECHOWSKI lives with her husband and three children in Pittsford, New York. *Patty Dillman of Hot Dog Fame* is her second book. Her first, *And the Other, Gold*, is also about Patty Dillman.

More Patty Dillman!
AND THE OTHER, GOLD
by Susan Wojciechowski

When eighth-grader Patty Dillman catches a football in the face, she never imagines that it will help her catch a boyfriend! But before she knows it, she and Tim—the thrower of the football (and a hunk!)—are quite an item. Patty is thrilled, and devotes her time—which used to be spent getting into trouble with her best friend, Tracy—talking to Tim, thinking about Tim, and daydreaming about Tim. So where does that leave Tracy? Patty won't even talk to Tracy on the phone, because Tim might be trying to call! Feeling left out and discouraged, Tracy begins to spend time with her friends from the school play—which makes Patty feel rejected! Can their friendship survive the greatest challenge known to teenage girls—the boyfriend?

"Refreshing and believable." —*Publishers Weekly*

"Likable and breezy." —*School Library Journal*

"Right on target!" —*Booklist*

BULLSEYE BOOKS PUBLISHED BY ALFRED A. KNOPF, INC.

Is there a trick to finding Mr. Right?

MARCI'S SECRET BOOK OF FLIRTING
(Don't Go Out Without It!)
by Jan Gelman

Now that they're in junior high, Marci and Pam know their dating careers should be starting. What they don't know is how to *get* them started. How will they actually meet boys? They decide to ask Marci's former baby-sitter, Cathy, for advice, and she comes through with flying colors. Soon Marci and Pam are learning how to flirt—with step-by-step instructions based on Cathy's expert research. The question is, will their new technique work on the cutest hunk in the seventh grade, Peter, and his blue-eyed buddy, Dave?

BULLSEYE BOOKS PUBLISHED BY ALFRED A. KNOPF, INC.

Why couldn't they just stay twelve forever?
THE TROUBLE WITH THIRTEEN
by Betty Miles

Annie and Rachel think life at twelve is just perfect. Even though all their friends are in such a hurry to grow up, wanting things like pierced ears and boyfriends, the two of them are happy with things the way they are. But things can't stay the same forever. First, Annie's beloved dog dies in her arms. Then, Rachel's parents decide to get a divorce, which means Rachel has to move to New York City with her mother. Annie is afraid that living in New York will turn Rachel into a stuck-up city girl, and Rachel is scared of losing her cherished position as Annie's best friend. But together Annie and Rachel learn a lot about independence and loyalty—and that there are, after all, some good things about turning thirteen.

"Authentic, balanced and believable...the book is a winner." —*School Library Journal*

"Solid gold!" —*Publishers Weekly*

BULLSEYE BOOKS PUBLISHED BY ALFRED A. KNOPF, INC.